The Horse
That Played
Center Field

The Horse That Played Center Field

Hal Higdon

SCHOLASTIC INC.
New York Toronto London Auckland Sydney Tokyo

ISBN 0-590-62011-8

12 11 10 9 8 7 6 5 4 3 2   4 5 6 7/8

Printed in the U. S. A.   06

To Rose,
mother of a real life Kevin

chapter 1

Kevin Darling almost fell off his horse when he saw the goat staring at him. The goat wore a baseball hat between his two horns. He grinned wickedly at Kevin.

The goat wasn't real. It was only the picture of a goat on a poster next to the baseball stadium in Chatahatchee, Florida. "TONIGHT," announced the poster in bright red letters, "THE NEW YORK GOATS."

Kevin dismounted to look at the poster more closely. Did the goat really play baseball? That would be worth seeing. Kevin turned toward Oscar, his horse, and looked puzzled. If Oscar knew the meaning of the poster, he didn't say.

Kevin had been riding into town to buy some nails at the hardware store so he and his father could repair the fence around their orange grove. To reach town he needed to pass the baseball stadium next door. That was when he spotted the poster.

"Golly, Oscar," Kevin said to his horse. "Maybe someone in town can tell us what the poster means." He started to remount.

At that moment the stadium janitor appeared. He carried a broom over one shoulder. The janitor looked like a soldier marching off to war. "Excuse me," Kevin said to him.

The janitor pulled the broom from his shoulder, ready to do battle. "What is it? What is it?" he snapped.

"Excuse me," repeated Kevin. "What are the New York Goats?"

The janitor leaned on the broom and gave the question some thought. He peered at Kevin and then at his horse. "Haven't you heard of the New York Goats? Why, they're a major league baseball team."

Then before Kevin could speak, the janitor suddenly raised an open palm like a policeman stopping traffic. He had a better idea.

"No," he said. "The New York Goats are a baseball team that *plays* in the major leagues!"

The janitor smiled, certain he had uttered a great truth. He placed his broom back on his shoulder and marched away into the ball park.

Kevin puzzled over what the janitor had said.

He watched the games of the local baseball team. They were the Alligators, not the Goats. The Chatahatchee Alligators ranked as the top team in the Class D Grapefruit League.

But Kevin didn't know much about the major leagues. According to the janitor, the New York Goats were *not* a major league baseball team. They were only a team that *played* in the major leagues. They were and they were not. That didn't make sense. It didn't even make nonsense.

The janitor had almost vanished under the stands. "My grandmother lives in New York," Kevin shouted after him.

The janitor stopped, turned, and fixed Kevin with one eye: "Does your grandmother know how to play center field?"

"No, she just sews."

"Too bad. If she played center field, she probably could get a job with the Goats." The janitor roared with laughter as he marched out of sight.

Kevin tried to imagine his grandmother circling under a fly ball. "I could write and ask her," he yelled after the janitor. But the man was no longer there.

Kevin glanced again at the poster showing the goat wearing a baseball hat. "I guess 'Goats' is only the name of the team," he said to Oscar, his horse. Kevin laughed at himself. Imagine, believing that an animal might play baseball. What a silly idea.

He rode Oscar at a gallop toward town. They stopped before the hardware store. In a big city like New York or Chicago, you wouldn't expect to see horses parked at the curb, but this was Chatahatchee, Florida. Kevin dismounted and told Oscar to wait.

He ran inside, letting the screen door bang behind him. "The Goats are coming," he announced.

The hardware-store owner peered at him through thick glasses. "I can sell you some fencing," he said.

"No," said Kevin. "The Goats are a major league team."

"In that case," said the store owner, "you may need barbed wire."

Kevin decided the store owner just didn't understand baseball. "I'll take a pound of large nails instead," he sighed.

When Kevin returned to the street, his horse had begun to prance up and down. Oscar whinnied for him to hurry. People crowded the street. Everyone seemed to be running the same way.

"Gee, Oscar, someone's house must be burning," said Kevin. But he hadn't heard any sirens.

Then Kevin saw Bill Redshield, sports editor of the Chatahatchee *News-Dispatch*. He was a jolly, red-faced man who was shaped somewhat like a beach ball—or Santa Claus. Redshield emerged from the newspaper office and stared after the crowd. Then he joined the rush. Tugging Oscar by the reins, Kevin ran after the sports editor, a good friend of his.

"Where is everyone going, Bill?" he asked.

"Down to the train depot," panted Redshield. "The New York Goats arrive on the noon train."

"Are the Goats a good baseball team?"

Bill Redshield seemed shocked by the question. He slowed and pulled a giant white handkerchief from his pocket. He wiped his brow.

"The Goats are the *worst* team in the major leagues," he said. "They've finished last every season. They've made more errors, allowed more runs, struck out more times, and lost more games than any other team in major league history. They're not just bad, they're awful!

"I could probably play center field for them," added Redshield.

"Gee, I hope not," Kevin said. "I hoped my grandmother might get that job."

The sports editor looked at Kevin and then shook his head. "Well, anybody would be better than their present center fielder," snorted Redshield. "Lefty Oliver! What a clod! Drops everything that falls near him. We could stick that horse of yours out in center field and he could catch more balls."

Kevin turned toward Oscar in surprise. Actually, Bill Redshield didn't know it, but his horse was a good catcher. Some horses like apples, but Oscar loved to eat oranges. At his father's orange grove, some of the workers would lob oranges at Oscar and the horse would catch them in his teeth. But Oscar had never caught a baseball. It was hard to picture him in a baseball uniform. Kevin remembered the goat on the poster and laughed.

"If they're so awful," Kevin asked the sports editor, "why is everyone hurrying to see them?"

Redshield halted to think. "I don't know," he finally replied. "I guess the Goats are just so awful that nobody believes it. So everyone has to come out and see for himself."

"Sort of like owning a skunk that smells worse than anything in the world," said Kevin.

"You know"—Redshield grinned—"you may be right."

chapter 2

Casey Balloo, manager of the worst baseball team in the history of the world, stepped from the train and took a deep breath of Florida air.

"Ahhh," said Casey, filling his lungs. "Just smell the scent of oranges."

"Oranges don't smell," snorted a stumpy man standing beside him. "I don't smell a thing." Arch Crabwheat, press secretary for the New York Goats, glared at the railroad station before him. He decided it had not been painted since the visit of Ponce de León.

"Take that foul cigar out of your mouth," said Casey. "Maybe then you could smell the oranges."

"One-two-three," a man in a red jacket chanted as he waved a baton over his head. The

Chatahatchee high school marching band began to play "Take Me Out to the Ball Game."

A cheer rose from the crowd. Kevin Darling strained on tiptoe to see over the people in front of him. Then he had a bright idea. He climbed on Oscar's back. From there he could see everything.

Bill Redshield tried to push his way through the crowd. He clutched a notebook in one round, red hand.

"Let me through. Let me through," he squealed. "Press! Press! Make way for the press!"

The band finished its number. The red-jacketed leader stuck his baton under one arm and turned to face the Goats' manager. "Welcome to Chatahatchee, Mr. Balloo," he said. "I'm Mayor O'Grady."

Casey Balloo offered him a gnarled hand. "That's quite a band you've got there, Mayor," said Casey with a wink. "The mayor of New York makes a lot of noise. But I can't recall having seen him lead his own band."

"Being mayor in Chatahatchee isn't a full-time job. I also teach music," answered Mayor O'Grady. He reached in his pocket for several sheets of paper. He began to read: "The people of Chatahatchee. . . ."

Casey Balloo pretended to listen to the welcome speech. Meanwhile he thought: how pleasant to be mayor of some small town, with nothing to do but meet trains and teach music. Maybe this fellow O'Grady would trade jobs with him. Casey could become mayor of Chatahatchee. The mayor could become manager of the Goats. He certainly could do no worse than Casey.

For four years Casey Balloo had managed the Goats into last place. They weren't a bad team. They were a *horrible* team! And they seemed to be getting worse. The worse they got, the louder the people of New York cheered—as though they loved a loser.

Casey couldn't understand it. Well, the hometown fans should be happy this year. This team played so poorly it had failed to win a single game during spring training. Not one!

That alone had prompted Casey Balloo to bring his world's worst team to Chatahatchee. Casey thought maybe they could win against a Class D minor league squad. Just one victory, that's all he wanted.

Casey almost dreaded returning to New York. Not that the fans disliked him. Casey could do no wrong in their eyes. Only the sports reporters bothered him. They wanted a winning team. And one reporter made more noise than all the rest: Phil Furlong of the New York

Bugle. Furlong had an acid pen. Casey shuddered at what he would write if they returned home from spring training with all losses on their record.

". . . hope you will enjoy your stay."

The mayor finished his speech and the crowd applauded. Meanwhile, Bill Redshield tried to push his way to the front. "Make way for the press," he pleaded, waving his notebook high over his head. "Press! Press! Reporter coming through."

Casey Balloo shook Mayor O'Grady's hand once more, waved at the crowd, then turned to Arch Crabwheat.

"I guess it's safe to bring them out now," he whispered.

Several pairs of eyes peeked fearfully from the railroad car doorway to assure themselves that no eggs would be thrown. Crabwheat motioned for the team to step from the train.

From his seat on horseback, Kevin spotted the baseball players first. "Look, Oscar," he said. "It's the New York Goats." The horse's ears perked up.

Indeed, it was the New York Goats. One by one they descended to the train platform.

First came Spider Switchstick, a narrow-shouldered man with legs like broom handles. He played shortstop for the Goats and last year set a major league record. Switchstick had allowed four ground balls to roll through his legs in one inning.

Yet on certain days Spider could field better than any shortstop in the league. Casey Balloo always believed he had talent. Maybe playing in front of too many people scared Spider, who came from a small town.

The next to step onto the platform was Fireball Smith, a pitcher with hair as bright as his nickname and a jaw hardened by thousands of plugs of chewing tobacco. Last season he led all National League pitchers in losses: twenty-four of them compared to only three wins.

"It takes skill to lose that often," claimed Fireball when he asked for a raise in pay after the season. "A really poor pitcher wouldn't play often enough to lose that many games." And Fireball was right. He had a great fast ball. He just couldn't get it over the plate often enough.

Mountain Malone lumbered from the train. He stood nearly seven feet tall and weighed three hundred pounds. He could hit long home runs, but more often he struck out. Malone had trouble hitting a curve. And his fielding was terrible! Phil Furlong once wrote of Malone: "He plays first base like a blindfolded man before a firing squad."

Following Malone was Tubby Swenton, the

catcher with the strongest arm in baseball. He proved this during one game last season. When a runner tried to steal second base, Swenton had thrown the ball into the third row of the center-field bleachers.

Then came Lefty Oliver, a tall, stringy center fielder. Lefty had trouble convincing people he was really right-handed. He had obtained his nickname because the sports reporters accused him of having two left feet.

One by one the New York Goats stepped onto the railroad platform and stood shyly staring at the crowd. It's not that they don't have talent, thought Casey. They had that. But each one also seemed to have at least one fatal flaw that prevented him from becoming a true major leaguer.

Casey Balloo looked at his forlorn crew. General Custer's army probably looked better after the battle of Little Big Horn. Casey swore this season would be his last. He wondered if they would let him manage his home-town Little League team after he retired.

The manager of the New York Goats threw one arm around Mayor O'Grady's shoulders. With his free hand, he brushed his silver hair away from his face. It was a very folksy gesture. He had picked it up watching the late movies on television.

"Ladies and Gentlemen of Chatahatchee,"

Casey began. "Thank you for welcoming us to your fine town. We hope to see all of you at the ball park tonight." Everyone applauded.

At that moment a round-faced man with a notebook in one hand finally wormed his way to the front of the crowd. He approached Lefty Oliver. "You're Oliver," he said. "I'm Redshield of the *News-Dispatch.*"

"Pleased to meet you, I'm sure," Lefty said.

Redshield thrust the notebook he had been carrying toward the Goats' center fielder. "I wonder if I could have your autograph?" he asked.

"Why sure," said Lefty Oliver. "Whoops!" He dropped the notebook on the ground.

"Don't take offense," growled Arch Crabwheat from the rear. "He drops practically everything." Lefty blushed and signed his name with his good right hand.

Casey Balloo walked toward the hotel followed by his team. Mayor O'Grady pumped his baton up and down, and from the Chatahatchee high school marching band came the strains of "Give My Regards to Broadway."

"This isn't such a bad town, Archibald," Casey said to his press secretary. "A man could buy himself an orange grove and sit in the sun for the rest of his life. You know, a man can't go on managing forever."

"Especially not with this team," snorted Arch Crabwheat.

Kevin waited until the crowd had gone, then whispered to his horse: "Okay, Oscar. Let's go home." The horse started down the street at a slow trot. In the excitement, Kevin had forgotten all about the nails he had bought for his father.

As he rode past the ball park where the Goats would play that night, he said to his horse: "Gee, Oscar. A team from the major leagues playing right here at the end of our orange grove."

Oscar whinnied. He seemed excited too.

When Kevin reached home, he jumped off his horse, letting Oscar run into the trees. Oscar nuzzled up to one of the hired hands, whinnied pleadingly, and opened his mouth. The hired hand laughed and threw him a fresh orange.

Kevin found his father standing at his work bench. Mr. Darling turned and frowned. "Well, where are the nails? Did you make each one by hand?"

Kevin threw the bag of nails on the bench. "Guess what's going to happen tonight?" he said.

His father looked at him without smiling. "The moon is going to turn into a pumpkin."

"The New York Goats are going to play in

town," said Kevin. "I've never seen a really good baseball team before."

"You still won't have seen one—even after tonight," grumbled his father. He reached inside his shirt pocket for a white envelope. He threw it onto the work bench.

The envelope contained three baseball tickets: one for Kevin, one for his father, and one for his mother.

"Hooray!" shouted Kevin. "We're going to the game." But then he became sad.

"What's wrong?" asked his father.

"You didn't get a ticket for Oscar."

Kevin's father laughed. "Who ever heard of a horse inside a baseball park?"

Who, indeed?

chapter 3

Early that evening the main street of Chatahatchee, Florida, closed up tighter than a tightwad's wallet. A sign in the window of the drug store explained why. "Gone to the ball game," it said.

The people of Chatahatchee headed toward the baseball park at the end of town next to the Darlings' orange grove. Men drove cars and trucks. Women pushed baby carriages. Kids pedaled bikes. Dogs and cats walked. "I haven't seen such bustle," one old timer said, "since the hurricane of '97."

Kevin's father donned a clean white shirt and a bow tie. His mother wore a flowered dress and tied a yellow ribbon in her hair. Kevin wore his newest pair of overalls. After everyone had dressed, they locked the front door and climbed into the family jeep.

Oscar stood nearby. He fixed Kevin with his sad, brown eyes. "I'd like to take you, Oscar," said Kevin, "but Dad says they don't let horses in ball parks."

Just at that minute a pink sports car stopped on the highway, blocking their driveway. Two men sat in the front seat, one wearing a derby pulled over one eye and a purple and yellow checked sports coat. The other wore a peach-colored vest and chewed on a toothpick.

"Hey, Mister," the driver of the sports car shouted to Kevin's father. "Which way to the ball park?"

Mr. Darling leaned his head out of the jeep. "Straight down the road," he said.

The pink sports car roared off, leaving a cloud of dust. "That's a seedy-looking pair," commented Kevin's mother.

"Probably fans of the Goats," said Kevin's father. "I noticed they have a New York license plate." He drove the jeep out of the driveway toward the baseball park.

Oscar watched the family go. Then he gave a snort and trotted to the end of the orange grove. The outfield fence was low enough for a tall horse to stick his nose over it. And Oscar was a tall horse.

Meanwhile, Mr. Darling parked his jeep near

the entrance to the park. "Get your score cards here," a vendor shouted as Kevin and his parents walked inside. "Can't tell the players without a score card."

"Gee, Dad. Shall we get a score card?" asked Kevin.

His father shrugged. "You've got your own money from doing the chores." Kevin reached into his pocket for a silver coin and paid the vendor.

"Baseball bats," hawked another vendor as they walked up the stairs into the stands. The vendor swung a handful of tiny bats over his head. "Get a bat autographed by the players."

"Just a minute, Dad. I'm going to buy a baseball bat too," said Kevin. He paid the man and discovered that his bat was autographed by Lefty Oliver.

"Baseball caps," shouted a third vendor as they sat down. "Just like those worn by the New York Goats."

"Gosh, those hats look cool . . ." began Kevin, reaching into his pocket for some more money.

"I hope the team isn't for sale," said his mother, "or you'll probably end up owning that too."

Suddenly the crowd roared as the New York Goats charged onto the field for their warm-up. At least everyone charged except Lefty Oliver.

He tripped on the top step of the dugout and sprawled on his face in the grass.

Lefty scrambled to his feet, dusted off his cap, and began to run again toward center field. Then he heard Casey Balloo bellow at him: "Oliver, you forgot something!"

Lefty stopped for a minute and scratched his head, trying to remember what he forgot.

"Your brains!" roared the Goats' manager and stalked off to the coach's box near first base.

Lefty Oliver's face became as red as the lettered name "Goats" on his chest. He turned and shuffled toward center field. Lefty noticed a large, friendly, tan-colored horse with its nose stuck over the fence.

"Hi, horse," said Lefty. "Looks like you have the best seat in the house."

The horse (who of course was Oscar) whinnied back.

Casey Balloo stood near first base with his arms folded across his chest and observed his team warming up. It reminded him of watching the Three Stooges on television. A ball thrown by shortstop Spider Switchstick sailed over first baseman Mountain Malone's head and into the grandstand. A fan sitting in a box seat speared it with one bare hand.

"Quick, sign that fan to a contract!" bellowed Casey. The crowd laughed. Casey responded by winking and flashing a devilish grin. You had to have a good sense of humor to manage the Goats.

Everyone knew Casey to be fast with a joke, one reason why he had his present job. A person who couldn't laugh would have gone crazy managing the collection of bums, misfits, has-beens, and never-will-bes that formed the roster of the New York Goats.

Baseball had been Casey Balloo's job almost all of his life—first as a player, then as a coach, and finally as a manager of the New York Bombers. The Bombers were the other baseball team in New York City. They played in the American League.

In a lifetime in the major leagues, Casey had played with or managed a dozen pennant winners. With him as manager, the Bombers had proved unbeatable.

Then one day near the end of a season when the team finished only third, the owner of the club called Casey into his office. He offered the manager a chair and a cigar.

Something is wrong, thought Casey. The chair is free, but the cigar costs money.

"Casey," said the owner. "We think you need a rest. You've worked hard for us. There comes a time in life when a man should slow down." What the owner meant was: Casey was fired.

The fans rebelled at seeing Casey go. They

turned the final day of the season into Casey Balloo Day. Sixty-five thousand people jammed the stands. When the owner of the team appeared in his box seat, he was booed.

The fans presented Casey with a new car, which he didn't need. They gave his wife a fur coat, which she didn't need. They should have had a rocking chair at home plate, thought Casey. That really was what he was getting.

The next season Casey puttered in his garden, raising roses, and watched the baseball games on television. He nearly died of boredom.

Then one day the phone rang. The man on the other end offered Casey a job the following year as manager. The National League had added two new teams. The New York entry would be called the Goats. The team consisted mostly of castoffs, players nobody else wanted.

"We may not win the pennant this first season," Casey admitted to reporters. "We're going to build for the future."

As it turned out, "the future" probably meant some time after the start of regular rocket service to the moon. The Goats lost more games than any other team in history during their first season in the league. Since then they had gotten worse.

Yet the fans loved Casey and refused to boo him. They jammed the ball park by the thousands, just to see their team lose in style. Anything the Goats did seemed fine with the New York fans. They even cheered errors and strike-outs.

That was part of the problem with the Goats. If a player gets cheered for playing badly, why bother to play well? Soon, whenever a Goats' player struck out or dropped a fly ball, he simply laughed. Why get angry when no one else did? At this point the Goats stopped being ballplayers and became clowns. Even the young, more talented ballplayers who joined the club adopted the comic ways of the other players.

So the Goats lost and lost and lost and lost and lost again. They ranked first in the hearts of their fans, but last in the National League.

Standing in the first-base coach's box in the Chatahatchee ball park, Casey watched a prac-tice ground ball bounce and hit his third base-man in the chin. He turned away, unable to watch anymore. Casey would like to win just one more pennant. Just one pennant—to prove he could still do it. Then he would gladly accept that rocking chair again.

."Play ball!" shouted the umpire.

The Chatahatchee Alligators ran onto the field. They were mostly plumbers, gas station mechanics, and orange grove workers who played baseball at night during their spare time.

The only way any of the Alligators would gain entry to a major league ball park was by buying a ticket at the door. Here, thought Casey, is a team we can beat.

"Who do you think will win?" Kevin asked his father while sitting in the stands.

"The Goats," said Mr. Darling. "They're from the majors. These local boys shouldn't have a chance."

But after the first three Goat batters failed to hit, the Alligators came to bat. Fireball Smith shifted the chaw of tobacco from one cheek to the other and glared at the plate as though he might melt it. He zipped three steaming strikes past the batter, but Tubby Swenton let the final one bounce away. The Alligator player sprinted to first base as Tubby scrambled after the ball, which was rolling toward the backstop.

"Safe on first," cried the umpire when Tubby failed to throw.

"I think the ball rolled into a gopher hole," Tubby explained.

The second Alligator batter dribbled a grounder toward the shortstop. Spider Switch-stick bent low and charged the ball like a bull enraged by a red cape. He reached low and speared the ball barehanded—a great play! Then he turned and threw to catch the runner sliding into second base. The ball sailed over the second baseman's head into center field. By the time center fielder Lefty Oliver retrieved it, Alligator runners stood on second and third.

Fireball Smith frowned. He threw four balls to the next batter to load the bases.

Then the Chatahatchee Alligators' clean-up batter stepped to the plate. Casey Balloo's eyes widened as he saw who it was: the same man who had greeted him at the station. Mayor O'Grady, band leader and clean-up batter, swung two bats over his shoulder. He threw one away and growled.

"Hit it out of the park, Mayor O'Grady," the fans shouted.

Mayor O'Grady adjusted the glasses on his nose. He pulled his cap low on his forehead. He scuffed the dirt with his gym shoes and swung with his eyes closed at the first pitch. *Crack!* The baseball flew high in the air along the right-field line.

The right fielder followed the ball with his eyes, going up, up, up, up, up, then down, down, down, down, down over the fence into the orange grove. A home run! The Alligators led the Goats 4 to 0.

Casey Balloo closed his eyes to be spared the sight of four men crossing the plate. "It's going to be a long, hot summer," he muttered to himself.

But the Goats refused to die. They scored

three runs in the second inning and two in the third. Then the Alligators knocked across three runs and the Goats got seven. Both teams continued to score. Fireball Smith left the game in the sixth inning after throwing fourteen balls in a row. His last pitch beaned a hot dog salesman in the grandstand.

"Hey, Casey," a fan shouted. "Last year a girls' softball team visited town, and they played better than your team!" Casey looked the other way. He knew it was true.

When the Goats took the field in the ninth inning, they led 17 to 14. And Kevin's horse Oscar still stood behind the center-field fence watching the game as the first two batters made outs. Oscar lifted his head as the Alligators' next batter popped a high fly ball toward the outfield. The ball game almost was over.

Lefty Oliver gritted his teeth and sprang into action at the crack of the bat. His tall shoulders arched. His sharp brown eyes narrowed as he focused on the flight of the ball. He moved two steps to his right. He darted to the left three steps. He backed up slowly and watched the fly ball descending toward him. Then he raised his mitt.

The ball hit him on the head.

Before the other fielder could retrieve the ball, the batter had a triple. Casey called time and strode crimson-faced into center field. Oliver sat dazed on the grass. He smiled weakly at his approaching manager.

"Oliver, you're—" sputtered Casey. "You're —" Then the Goats' manager noticed Oscar leaning over the center-field fence. Casey pointed at the horse. "Oliver, that horse can probably play better center field than you!"

Suddenly a light glowed in Casey Balloo's eyes. A devilish grin swept his face. Well, why not, he thought angrily. Maybe it would teach these clowns a lesson. The umpire meanwhile had strolled into center field.

Casey spun and faced him. "Would you object if I used a player not on our roster?"

"It's only a practice game," shrugged the umpire. "Suit yourself."

"All right," said Casey. "That horse is playing center field!" He leveled a stubby finger at Oscar.

"Golly snapdragons," shouted Kevin, leaping from his seat in surprise. "That's Oscar!" He was watching Casey Balloo lead Oscar through a large gate in the outfield fence. The manager stationed the horse in center field and walked back to his coaching position. When the crowd realized what was happening, it roared with laughter.

"Now playing in center field," crackled the loudspeaker, "an unknown horse."

"That's no unknown horse," said a stunned Kevin. "That's Oscar! He's playing center field."

All his father could do was groan and stare. "The whole world has gone mad," he finally said.

Kevin's mother shook her head. "Well, Oscar can't do much worse than that Lefty Oliver fellow."

The Goats' pitcher scowled at his manager. "What's the big idea of putting a horse out in center field?"

"You just pitch to the batter," snapped Casey. "Throw hard enough and it won't matter if the Fifth Cavalry Division is backing you up."

The pitcher threw the next pitch hard. And the pitch after that. And the next six pitches. All of them were balls and the bases were again loaded.

"Get the ball over the plate," moaned Casey. He would have put in another pitcher, but he didn't have any more. The pitcher glowered and threw. The ball floated over the plate looking fat as a rubber life raft. *Smack!* The crowd jumped to its feet as they saw the ball rocket straight toward center field.

In the dugout Casey Balloo turned white. Why did he allow himself to get angry enough to put a horse in center field? The Alligators' base runners streaked for home. Now they would score four runs. He'd lose the one ball game the Goats had a chance to win all spring. "What have I done to myself?" he groaned.

Out in center field Kevin's horse nibbled the outfield grass. Looking up, Oscar saw the baseball heading straight toward him. It was small and round. Except for being white, it looked just like an orange. So Oscar lifted his head and caught the baseball in his teeth.

It took a good ten seconds before Casey Balloo's dropped jaw would move. "I don't believe it," he said.

And up in the stands neither did two seedy-looking men, one wearing a derby, the other chewing a toothpick.

chapter 4

The next morning manager Casey Balloo scanned both the Miami and New York papers at breakfast. He smiled when he found only a single line about last night's game. The papers had simply listed the score.

Nobody knew a horse had made the last put-out. None of the big-city reporters had come with them to Chatahatchee. Casey wouldn't tell them what they missed.

"If Phil Furlong knew what happened last night, he'd roast me in print," Casey said to himself.

The Goats' manager squeezed his breakfast grapefruit over a spoon. He made a sour face as he swallowed the juice. A horse playing base-ball! He wanted to forget what happened last night. So the horse had caught the ball. It was an accident. It would never happen again in one hundred years.

Casey regretted using the horse. He wouldn't have done it if Lefty Oliver hadn't made him so mad. He made a mistake like that once before.

Two years ago, near the end of the season, the Goats had sunk forty games out of first place. Then press secretary Arch Crabwheat came to Casey one day. "How does this idea grab you?" Arch asked.

Crabwheat wanted to sponsor a contest for their fans. The winner could manage the team for a day. Casey had agreed to the idea. They held the contest and a Brooklyn garbage collector won. He became manager one Sunday afternoon in September. Casey sat in the stands and watched.

That day, with the garbage collector as manager, the Goats won. This broke a seven-game losing streak. It was a double-header, so Arch Crabwheat said: "Let the guy manage the second game." Casey shrugged and returned to his seat in the stands.

The Goats won the second game and the fans carried the garbage collector off the field on their shoulders. They'd cheer the devil himself if he could win ball games.

At the end of a week the team had won seven games in a row for their new manager. *Time* magazine carried the garbage collector's picture on its cover. Sports writers began to talk about naming him manager of the year. Hollywood wanted to do a movie. One company started to sell garbage cans with the man's name signed on the lids. Casey decided this would be a good time to retire.

But then the Goats lost the next seven games. The fans booed the garbage collector when he came on the field. Hollywood canceled plans for the movie. Nobody bought his signed garbage cans anymore. Finally the garbage collector quit. "I'd rather collect garbage than manage a team like this," he told Casey. And that's just what he did.

Recalling the events of two years ago made Casey shudder. He paid for his breakfast and walked out into the hotel lobby. Arch Crabwheat, a long cigar stuck in his mouth, was waiting.

"Casey, I've found him," said Crabwheat, flicking ashes from his cigar onto the hotel rug. "Here's the young man who will make the Goats famous."

Casey frowned. Crabwheat's idea of fame and Casey's idea of fame were not the same. Casey gazed at the skinny young man standing next to the press secretary. It was Kevin Darling. Kevin grinned at him.

"Well, if he wants to try out with the team
——" began the Goats' manager.

"Casey, the lad doesn't play baseball," said
Crabwheat. "His horse does."

Casey Balloo pictured in his mind a baseball
dropping into the mouth of the horse in center
field. It was a picture he wanted to forget.

"Look, Archibald, it was a fluke," said the
Goats' manager. "So the horse caught the ball.
It couldn't happen again."

Kevin looked hurt. "But gee, Mr. Balloo," he
began. "Oscar's a fine catcher. Honest! He's
been catching oranges for years."

Casey Balloo placed one palm on his chest
and pointed his other hand at the ceiling. He
had learned this pose also while watching the
late movies on television. He used the pose each
season when he told sports writers that his team
would win the pennant.

"Oranges are not baseballs," intoned the
manager of the New York Goats.

Arch Crabwheat grinned and bit down on his
cigar. "Look, Casey, I didn't believe it at first
either." The press secretary gripped the manager by one arm and whispered in his ear. "This
morning I rose early and went out to find the
horse. His name's Oscar. He belongs to the lad
here."

Casey looked sternly at Kevin as though
aware of Crabwheat's plans.

"Archibald," began Casey, "a horse that catches oranges might do fine on the Ed Sullivan TV Show, but not in a major league baseball park."

But Crabwheat motioned for Casey to follow him outside.

Oscar stood in the street in front of the hotel. He whinnied when he saw the Goats' manager approach.

"The same to you, I'm sure," grumbled Casey.

"Now watch this," said Crabwheat. "Let's see if that catch last night was a fluke or not."

The press secretary reached into his coat and produced a baseball. Casey applauded him. "Bravo," he said. "That's almost as good as pulling a rabbit out of a hat."

"No jokes now," said Crabwheat. He moved back two paces, then threw the ball underhand toward the horse. Oscar caught it easily in his mouth.

"Hmmmm," said Casey.

Crabwheat retrieved the ball from the horse and threw it to him a second time. Oscar caught it again.

"Hmmmm," repeated Casey. He took the baseball and threw it several times to the horse. Each time Oscar caught the ball perfectly in his teeth.

"I'll admit the horse does catch better than

Oliver," Casey finally admitted. "But he can't throw, can he?"

"He can run," said Kevin.

Casey snorted. "So can the winner of the Kentucky Derby, but he's not playing baseball for me."

"But, Casey," said Crabwheat. "What a great gimmick: a horse playing center field for the Goats. People would come from hundreds of miles to see it. Didn't Bill Veeck once send a midget to bat in St. Louis? What happened there?"

"He got a base on balls," snapped Casey. "But look, Arch, at least a midget can hold a bat, even if it's only a midget bat. Can a horse do that?"

Crabwheat nodded. "I'm glad you mentioned that." The press secretary motioned to Kevin. The boy reached into Oscar's saddle bag and found the half-sized bat he had purchased the night before. Kevin gave the bat to Oscar, who held it in his teeth.

"I don't believe it. I don't believe it," muttered Casey Balloo.

Arch Crabwheat handed Casey the baseball again. "Go on, test him," he said.

Casey stared with mouth agape at the horse gripping the bat in his teeth. "I grant you that the horse can catch. I agree that he can run."

Casey shook his head as though unwilling to believe his next thought.

"I've been working with Oscar since dawn," explained Kevin. "I admit he doesn't hit very well—yet."

"Go on," prodded Crabwheat. "Test him."

Casey Balloo stared angrily at his press secretary. He turned toward Oscar, who still stood with the bat held jauntily in his teeth. Finally Casey gripped the baseball and threw it toward the horse.

Oscar dropped the bat from his mouth and caught the ball.

"Ha ha!" shouted Casey in triumph. "Ha ha!" He turned and strode toward the entrance to the hotel.

"But, Casey," said Crabwheat, running after him.

"Ha ha!" repeated Casey. "You can lead a horse to water, but you can't make him hit!"

"But Lefty Oliver can't hit," snorted Crabwheat. "In fact, neither can Spider Switchstick, or Tubby Swenton, or Mountain Malone, or anybody else on the team."

Casey Balloo raised his eyes toward heaven as though searching for a friendly lightning bolt to strike him.

"Look, Case," said Crabwheat, putting one arm around the manager's shoulders. "I'm not asking you to play Oscar every game. But maybe some day when you're ten runs behind. It won't hurt. And the fans will love it. Just for one game, as a gag."

"That's what you said about that garbage collector," Casey replied.

"But, Casey," said the press secretary, "Oscar doesn't want to manage. He just wants to play center field. Clown it up a bit. The fans will love it."

Casey grew serious. "I think sometimes that's just what's wrong with this team," he said. "Too much clowning. All right. Bring the horse to New York. But I'll tell you when I'll play him— *if* I play him."

The Goats' manager walked inside the hotel. Arch Crabwheat turned to Kevin Darling and shook his hand. "We'll arrange to get you and Oscar to New York."

"I've got a grandmother who lives in New York," said Kevin. "I could live with her."

The two parted. Kevin mounted Oscar and rode home to his family's orange grove. The scene at the hotel, however, had been witnessed by two men: one wearing a derby, the other chewing a toothpick. They were Crooknose Jake and Louie the Skunk, two criminals who lived by betting on sporting events.

"What do you think, Jake?" asked Louie the Skunk.

"I think we should watch and wait," said the other man.

"I've been looking for a way to get even with Casey Balloo ever since he turned us in to the cops for trying to bribe one of his players. This may be our chance."

His partner nodded.

chapter 5

On the first day of the season the sun shone brightly on Goats Stadium. Fans began arriving early. Casey Balloo walked through the clubhouse tunnel to the playing field. He took a deep breath of the cool spring air and smiled.

"Even the smog tastes good today," said Casey.

Kevin Darling stood near the batting cage wearing a Goats' uniform with the numeral "0" on his back. Arch Crabwheat had appointed him batboy. "Good morning, Mr. Balloo," said Kevin.

"Morning Kevin," responded the manager. "A lovely day to begin the season."

"Oscar says hello too," began Kevin. "He's outside the ———"

Casey raised one finger to his lips. "Let's not say anything about your horse now," whispered the Goats' manager. "He's our secret."

"Okay, Mr. Balloo," agreed Kevin.

Casey patted Kevin on the shoulder and moved up the first-base line. He would just as soon forget the horse. Maybe Crabwheat would do the same, and they could quietly return Oscar to Florida. As soon as they saw Casey, a group of reporters who had been waiting near the dugout moved toward him.

"Hey, Chief," shouted one of the reporters. "Will you have a word with the press?"

Casey turned and shuddered. The voice belonged to Phil Furlong, sports writer for the New York *Bugle*. In his sports column, Furlong always spoke poorly of Casey and the Goats. After almost every game, Furlong wrote how poorly the team played. He said the team belonged in the minor leagues.

"The sun was shining until I saw you, Furlong," roared Casey. Despite Furlong's acid pen, Casey liked him. He enjoyed sparring with the reporter. Several writers from other papers gathered around to watch the duel.

"In what place will the Goats finish?" asked Furlong. "Or should I ask—in what league?" The other reporters chuckled at the remark.

"Well, boys," began Casey. "I believe the Goats will win the pennant."

"Come on, Casey," said Furlong. "The only way the Goats will ever win a pennant is by saving green stamps."

"Now don't be hasty," lectured Casey. He pointed toward Mountain Malone in the practice batting cage. "I think we have a fine club. Mountain Malone is the strongest batsman in the league."

As if Malone heard him, the big first baseman popped a practice pitch over the right-field wall.

"Malone can't hit a curve," said Furlong.

Casey ignored the remark. "And Fireball Smith can outthrow any pitcher."

"Can't find the plate," remarked Furlong.

"Now take Spider Switchstick," said Casey.

"Not with his fielding average, I won't," retorted Furlong.

"Now don't run down Switchstick," warned Casey. "Remember, he's kind to his mother."

Casey started to walk away, but couldn't avoid one last question. "Hey, Casey," Furlong added. "Someone said that in one game down in Florida you played a horse in center field."

The manager raised his eyebrows as though the news came as a surprise. He paused, then said: "Some of the boys down in Florida drank a little too much—uh, orange juice."

Before the laughter had died, Casey excused himself and walked toward the box seats. He found Arch Crabwheat chewing on a cigar. "They're on to us," said Casey. "They've heard about Oscar."

"Fine," said Crabwheat. "We've got the horse outside the left-field wall, where we keep the tractors. Just say the word and he'll come in to play."

Casey Balloo winced. "No, I don't want him to play. I want him on the next train back to Florida."

"Relax, Casey," said Crabwheat. "The club owner says he likes the idea of playing a horse in center field. He thinks it's a good gag. No hurry. Whenever you think the time is right."

Casey closed his eyes and wondered why he had put that horse in the game in Florida. Now he was stuck.

"All right," he told Crabwheat angrily. "But only in a game that's as good as lost."

Casey started to walk away. "If anyone asks about Oscar," Crabwheat called after him, "I'll tell them he's the team mascot."

At one o'clock the Goats ran from the dugout to take the field against the Chicago Bruins. Fireball Smith strode to the mound. "Play ball!" shouted the umpire. Smith rocked back and threw.

Thwump! Swish! Catcher Tubby Swenton had the ball in his mitt even before the batter completed his swing. "Strike one!" said the umpire.

Casey Balloo stood on the steps of the dugout and shook his head. Fireball Smith was fast. He could be a great pitcher. But sooner or later during each game he lost his confidence—and with it, his control.

And that's exactly what happened. In the fifth inning Tubby Swenton dropped a called third strike, allowing the batter to reach first base. Fireball walked the next two batters, and the following one hit a single, scoring two runs. The game ended with a 2 to 0 score. In the next two days, Chicago won two more games to sweep the series.

The Goats traveled out of town the following day to meet the Pittsburgh Pythons, but Kevin remained in New York. He had moved in with his grandmother. Oscar stayed in a livery stable near Goats Stadium.

"Can't Oscar go with the team?" Kevin asked Arch Crabwheat.

Crabwheat bit down on his cigar. "He wouldn't fit in the team airplane," said the press secretary. "When the Goats get home, I'm sure Oscar will play." The truth was that Casey Balloo still wanted Crabwheat to return the horse to Florida.

In Pittsburgh the Goats dropped three

games, one by a 14 to 3 score. Then they lost two in Philadelphia and one in Chicago. Returning home, the Goats faced the Pythons again. They lost two more games, their tenth and eleventh losses, before finally winning 7 to 6 in the twelfth inning.

"GOATS START WINNING STREAK," said the headlines on the sports page of the New York *Bugle* the next morning.

Then the Los Angeles Mules came to town and drubbed the Goats in three games. In Houston and then in Atlanta, the Goats lost all six games. They returned home dragging their bats behind them. They stood tenth and last in the National League, having won only one game while losing twenty. Next they had three games scheduled with the world champions, the St. Louis Birds. They lost the first two.

Before the third game with St. Louis, Casey slumped in an easy chair in the Goats' club house.

"One and twenty-two," he said, shaking his head. "This is the worst start yet. Maybe we do need a horse in center field."

Arch Crabwheat overheard but said nothing. Later, however, he called Kevin Darling over to his box seat.

"He's weakening," said Crabwheat. "He's weakening."

"Does that mean Oscar can play today?" asked Kevin.

"I'm not sure," answered the press secretary. "But be ready to bring him in. And be careful if you do. I don't want any peanut vendors trampled."

Fireball Smith started the game for the Goats. He stood on the mound rubbing the ball with one hand. Then he looked toward his catcher for the sign.

Tubby Swenton signaled for a fast ball and Smith nodded his agreement. Smith wound up and fired his fast ball straight over the plate. *Kuh-wack!* The batter hit the ball back so hard it almost took Smith's hat off.

The Birds scored three runs in the first inning. But Fireball Smith always pitched better when behind—as though he were afraid of winning. His fast ball came alive and he struck out thirteen Birds' batters. His teammates could only get one lone run, however. At the start of the ninth inning, the Birds still led the Goats 3 to 1.

With none out in the ninth, the first Birds' batter hit a pop fly that sailed lazily up into the air between left and center field. Lefty Oliver gritted his teeth and started to run toward left. At the same time the Goats' left fielder gritted his teeth and started to run toward center.

Bong! The two collided.

By the time the left fielder picked himself up and threw the ball in, the Birds' batter stood on second base. Lefty just lay there on the grass.

Unable to contain himself, Casey Balloo stormed onto the top step of the dugout and shouted toward his center fielder: "Oliver, a horse could play center field better than —" Then he stopped.

The Goats' manager turned around toward the box seats and saw Arch Crabwheat sitting in the first row. Crabwheat didn't say anything. He merely nodded his head.

Casey Balloo flushed. He felt like a man pursued by bloodhounds who runs into a dead-end alley. He first looked at Crabwheat, then gazed at the grandstands. A good number of the fans had already given up and gone home. Well, if it had to happen some day, why not today?

"Today?" Casey asked Crabwheat.

The press secretary merely nodded his head one more time.

Casey shrugged his shoulders and headed toward home plate. "Oscar playing center field," said the manager, at the same time pulling out a pencil to mark his score card.

"Oscar who?" asked the umpire.

"Just Oscar," said Casey and winked.

Up in the stands, Crooknose Jake and Louie

the Skunk sat next to one of their gambling friends. "What's the delay?" said the friend.

"Probably something silly," said Crooknose Jake slyly. "Maybe they're going to play a horse in center field."

"That's a joke," said the gambler.

"I've got a hundred bucks that says it's not," said Jake. He winked at his partner, Louie the Skunk.

"That'll be the easiest money I've ever made," said the gambler. "I'll take the bet!"

Meanwhile Kevin had run along the left-field line to the tractor gate. "Come on, Oscar," he yelled, and swung the gate open. Out trotted the horse. Oscar pranced and danced on his way to center field as though proud to be a Goat.

At first the crowd seemed too stunned to react. Then when they noticed that the horse wore a Goats' baseball cap—with holes cut in it so his ears fit through—they burst into laughter.

"Leave it to old Casey," roared the fans. They slapped one another on the back. "Even Bill Veeck never tried a stunt like this."

"What is this," rumbled the umpire, "some kind of bad joke?"

Casey smiled weakly. He turned and headed back toward the dugout. The four umpires clustered around home plate. One of them produced a rule book and began thumbing through its pages. Gales of laughter swept the stands.

One person didn't think it so funny, however. Fireball Smith's face turned red as his hair. "Daggone it," he growled at his manager. "This is no time for a joke."

"This whole team is a joke," Casey snapped back. "Shut up and pitch!"

The Goats' manager stalked back toward the dugout. At that moment Phil Furlong leaned over the railing and shouted at him: "Hey, Casey, what have you been drinking lately?"

"Orange juice," bellowed Casey Balloo, and went below.

Finally the umpires broke up their huddle. The plate umpire made a sign of helplessness. "Play ball!" he shouted. "Men, and *others!*"

Up in the stands the gambler friend of Crooknose Jake grumbled, "All right. You won the bet. You must have known Casey planned a stunt like this."

"It wasn't fair, I'll admit," said Crooknose Jake sweetly. "Tell you what. I'll give you a chance to win your money back. I'll bet the horse catches the first ball hit to him. Double or nothing."

"You're on," said the other gambler.

The next Birds' batter stood at the plate. He looked past the pitcher toward the horse in center field and started laughing. Fireball Smith tightened his belt. He rocketed two called strikes past the plate before the batter could stop laughing. The batter finally swung at the next pitch and dribbled a grounder to Spider Switchstick. The Goats' shortstop pounced on the ball and threw quickly to first base. But Mountain Malone fumbled it and runners were safe at first and third.

The Birds' first-base coach shouted at Casey: "You haven't got a cow you'd like to try on first, have you?" Mountain Malone turned purple.

Fireball Smith's shoulders slumped. He walked the next batter, loading the bases. "Well, at least our new center fielder hasn't made an error yet," grumbled Casey.

The Birds' clean-up batter appeared at the plate next. He was a man with a .342 batting average. He already had hit one home run that day. "I see a nice empty spot in center field where I can hit that ball," he told Tubby Swenton. And hit it he did. *Crack!* The ball headed high out over second base toward Oscar, who was grazing the outfield grass.

The minute the ball left the bat, all three base runners started to sprint. The first runner crossed the plate laughing as hard as he could. Then he turned to wave his teammates on. The second runner rounded third.

He had almost crossed the plate when Oscar lifted his head and calmly caught the ball.

For an instant no one in the ball park moved

or said a word. It was as if someone had pulled the TV set cord out of the wall. Suddenly the voice of one of the Birds' runners broke the silence: "Holy Oats! The horse caught it!"

The Birds' third-base coach realized his base runners stood at home plate—and the ball had been caught. "Get back!" he shouted. "Get back to your bases!"

But too late. The Goats' left fielder grabbed the ball from Oscar and rifled it to Spider Switchstick in the infield. The Goats' shortstop stared at the ball in his mitt for a second, as though not knowing what to do. Then he tagged second and threw the ball to first. A triple play!

Up in the stands, Crooknose Jake collected his money, then nudged his partner, Louie the Skunk. "We're going to make some more money off that horse," he cackled.

"How?" asked his partner.

"Just wait and watch," said Jake. "And we'll get even with Casey too."

Mountain Malone stalked in from first base and threw his fielder's mitt into the dugout. "Man, we don't need a horse to win games for us!"

Casey Balloo fixed him with an icy stare. "If you bat this inning, you can prove it!"

For a moment Kevin thought the giant first baseman meant Casey harm. Malone stood with his chest hardly two inches from the manager's chin. Then he sat down and started pounding his fist into his palm.

The first Goats' batter lifted an easy fly to left field for one out. A pinch hitter for Fireball Smith struck out. Then Spider Switchstick beat out an infield hit. The next batter walked.

When Mountain Malone stomped up to the plate, there were two men on base, two outs, and the Goats still trailed 3 to 1.

The Birds' pitcher smiled at the sight of the batter standing before him. Every pitcher in the league knew Malone was a sucker for a curve. The first pitch curled around the outside corner of the plate letter-high. "Stee-rike one," said the umpire. Malone just frowned.

A second curve broke even more sharply than the first. "Stee-rike two," announced the umpire. Malone just gritted his teeth.

The Birds' pitcher wiped his brow. He tugged at his cap. Once again the pitch came curving across the corner of the plate. But there was no call from the umpire. Instead there was a sharp *Cuh-rack*.

The Birds' pitcher looked up to see the baseball hit by Mountain Malone streak straight over his head. It was still going up when it cleared the center-field wall. Three men crossed the plate and the Goats won 4 to 3.

Casey Balloo stood on the edge of the dugout, his mouth as wide open as the Grand Canyon. "I don't believe it," he said. "I've seen triple plays. I've seen horses catch baseballs. But Mountain Malone hit a curve—never!"

chapter 6

The next morning Fireball Smith stormed into the Goats' club house waving a copy of the New York *Bugle* over his head. Kevin saw the angry look on his face and retreated to a corner. Fireball looked around the room until he spotted Mountain Malone. He threw the newspaper down on the bench beside the big first baseman.

"Look at this," snarled Smith.

"Well, I'll be fried," mumbled Malone.

The headline on the sports page said: "HORSE LEADS GOATS TO WIN OVER BIRDS."

Fireball Smith snapped his fingers angrily. "Nothing about the thirteen batters I struck out! Nothing about your home run in the ninth!

All the talk about is that doggone horse in center field."

"Well, I'll be fried!" repeated Malone.

Fireball Smith started to read the story aloud to him. Tubby Swenton and Spider Switchstick came over to listen. They frowned as Fireball read:

"Yesterday in Goats Stadium, Manager Casey Balloo learned that animals make better ballplayers than people. With his team losing to the St. Louis Birds by two runs in the ninth inning, Balloo sent a horse into center field to play.

"The horse, named Oscar, started a triple play to spike a Birds' rally. That seemed to ignite the home team. They scored three runs to win the game.

"No one knows where the horse came from, or where he learned to catch baseballs. It is something few other Goats' players can do."

"That's an insult!" said Tubby Swenton.

"It sure is!" grumbled Spider Switchstick.

"Well, I'll be *fried!*" said Mountain Malone once more.

Fireball Smith angrily threw the paper down on the floor and kicked it out of sight.

At that moment Casey Balloo entered the club house trailed by a dozen reporters. "How about it, Casey?" asked one reporter. "Do you plan to start that horse in center field today?"

"Or maybe you have an ape from the zoo as your starting pitcher," said Phil Furlong. The rest of the reporters laughed.

Casey smiled at them. "Of course I'll start Oscar," he said. "We've got a winning streak going. You don't change horses in the middle of the streak."

At that moment Lefty Oliver hobbled into the club house on crutches. He had a cast on one leg. "What's wrong, Lefty?" asked Furlong. "Did you fall off a horse?"

Lefty glared at the reporter as though tempted to hit him with a crutch.

Casey answered instead. "Lefty broke his leg colliding with the left fielder yesterday. He'll be out of the line-up for a couple of months."

"Who'll take his place?"

"Oscar, of course," said Casey.

"How does Lefty feel about that?" asked Furlong.

Lefty sat down on a bench and leaned his crutches across one knee. "I guess I'll visit the race track and find myself a jockey," he growled.

Casey noticed Kevin standing in one corner of the club house. "Fellows, meet Oscar's trainer," said Casey. "His name is Kevin Darling."

The reporters quickly turned from Casey.

They fired their questions at Kevin. "Where did your horse learn baseball?" asked one. "Has he played in the pony leagues?" Furlong asked.

The questions came so rapidly they made Kevin's head swim. "Gee, we never knew Oscar played baseball before this year," he explained. "He never told us."

Casey Balloo sneaked away from the group and headed toward his office. Furlong followed him. "Casey, do you really plan to keep the horse?" he asked. "I mean, a gag is a gag."

"We've got a winning streak," repeated the manager.

"A winning streak?" said the reporter. "You can't call one game a winning streak."

"To the Goats, one game is a winning streak," said Casey.

"What do the other players think of their new teammate?" asked Furlong.

Casey paused at the door to his office. "When you recall how many games they won *without* the horse," said the manager, "it doesn't matter what they think."

Later, Casey donned his baseball uniform and walked onto the field to watch batting practice. The fans already crowded the park. Having read in the paper about the horse that played center field, they wanted to see him. In the bleachers some fans had draped a sign over the wall. "THE BEST GOAT IS A HORSE," it said.

Then the crowd started to cheer. Oscar appeared at the tractor gate. He trotted toward the batting cage. Another sign fluttered down from the upper deck: "NO MORE NON-SENSE. HORSE SENSE." Casey looked up at it and smiled. His team might not be happy, but the fans were.

The manager of the San Francisco Owls walked over to the batting cage and stood near Casey. "I read about it in the papers," he said, "but I still don't believe it."

Casey Balloo winked at the other manager. "That horse will be rookie of the year," boasted Casey. "Of course, he's a little young: only three years old. But he has a great baseball future."

The Owls' manager watched Oscar step up to the plate carrying the midget bat in his teeth. The batting practice pitcher threw two balls past his nose. Oscar just sniffed at them. He swung at the next pitch and missed. "Harrumph," snorted the Owls' manager. "That horse can't hit."

Kevin Darling stood nearby. "Don't give up on Oscar," said Kevin. "He plays best under pressure." In the batting cage, Oscar nodded his head as if he understood them.

The Owls' manager harrumphed once more

and returned to the visiting team's dugout. "The next thing you know, they'll be asking Lassie to umpire," he complained.

Casey Balloo started to laugh. He put one hand on Kevin's shoulder. "I'm beginning to like the idea of a horse in center field," he said. "I'm having more fun than any time in the last four years."

But up in the stands two of Casey's enemies were trying to make some money. Crooknose Jake and Louie the Skunk stood talking to another gambler.

"I'd like the Goats to win today," said Jake.

"With a horse playing center field?" said the other gambler. "Don't be silly. What you saw yesterday was a fluke."

"Put your money where your mouth is," said Louie.

"You're on," said the other gambler. "Fifty dollars says the Goats lose."

Oscar trotted out to center field at the start of the game, and sixty thousand fans cheered. He had become a hero overnight.

The horse played well. He caught three fly balls for outs. On one bounce he fielded a line drive that might have gone for extra bases. After each catch Oscar would run into the infield with the ball. Oscar could catch, but of course he couldn't throw. For seven innings the Goats held the Owls scoreless.

The Goats also failed to score. Oscar struck out every time. All the other team's pitcher needed to do was lob the ball over the plate.

In the last of the eighth, Tubby Swenton opened the inning by getting a base on balls. He waddled to first base. The catcher with the large belly rated as perhaps the slowest man in baseball.

Oscar was up next. He stood clutching his midget bat in his teeth. The Owls' pitcher smiled and threw two easy strikes past him.

Tubby Swenton took several steps away from first base. The Owls' pitcher never looked at him. Of course not. None of the pitchers in the league watched Tubby when he was on base. He was so slow he had never even *tried* to steal a single base.

Tubby thought to himself: maybe it was time to start.

Just before the pitcher threw the ball Tubby dug for second. He ran with all the grace of a boulder rolling down a mountain. "Stee-rike three," said the umpire. Oscar was out, but Tubby Swenton slid safely into second with a stolen base. The Owls' catcher stood with the ball still in his mitt, too surprised to throw.

In the dugout Casey Balloo arched his eyebrows in wonder. Then Spider Switchstick moved to the plate swinging two bats. "Get mad, baby!" Mountain Malone bellowed at him. "Get mad!"

Switchstick threw one of the bats away. He reached down for some dirt and rubbed it into his hands. He pulled the plastic batting cap tight over his head. He glowered at the pitcher. On second base, Tubby Swenton took a long lead-off as though daring anyone to throw him out.

Switchstick watched two pitches sail past him for a ball and a strike. On the third pitch he whipped his bat around in an even arc. *Smack!* He hit the ball in a straight line toward the outfield. The right fielder dove for it and missed.

Meanwhile Tubby Swenton rounded third, digging for home. The Owls' center fielder picked up the rolling ball and rifled it toward home plate. With Tubby still ten feet from the plate, the ball slapped into the catcher's mitt.

Tubby didn't even bother to slide. He ran straight into the Owls' catcher. *Guh-voom!* There was a jarring crash. The two baseball players tumbled over each other in a cloud of dust and the ball popped out of the catcher's mitt. "Safe!" shouted the umpire.

Tubby limped proudly back to the dugout. Goats' players swarmed around him. "We showed that horse," laughed Mountain Malone. "I guess we showed him!"

Casey Balloo said nothing. He simply stood at one corner of the dugout with a puzzled look on his face. He had never seen his team act like this before.

The Owls went down in order in the ninth inning and the Goats won 1 to 0. The team ran down the left-field line toward the club-house door laughing and shouting after their victory. A few of them shook their fists angrily at Oscar, as though by winning they had proved something.

Casey Balloo trotted after them. Just before entering the club house, he spotted Phil Furlong. Casey wagged his finger at the reporter. "Now we really do have a winning streak."

chapter 7

The following day the Goats played San Francisco again. Oscar caught every ball hit near him. He also failed to hit.

It didn't matter. Hits bounced off the bats of his teammates like fruit out of an apple tree struck by lightning. The Goats scored so often they got dizzy circling the bases. When the other team batted, the Goats played without error. They made diving catches of sure hits. The Goats won 12 to 3.

"HORSE-LED TEAM GAINS ANOTHER VICTORY," said the sports page headlines.

This irked the Goats' players. "Horse-led team!" growled Mountain Malone. "We'll show them who's leading whom!"

"That afternoon the angry Goats played even harder and won by a 17 to 1 score. The headlines in the paper announced their victory: "WITH OSCAR IN CENTER GOATS CAN'T LOSE."

This made the Goats still madder. They drubbed the next team they played 23 to 0.

After the game, the players demanded a meeting. They didn't invite Oscar or Kevin. Fireball Smith rose to complain: "We're tired of playing second fiddle to a horse."

"That's right," added Mountain Malone. "We drive in all the runs. He simply cools it in center field and gets all the credit."

"He's making us look like clowns," grumbled Tubby Swenton. "It's not right for a horse to play baseball."

"Besides," suggested Spider Switchstick, "if we go on a road trip, who will room with *him?*"

Casey Balloo stood shaking his head. "Until last week, you bums couldn't outscore your grandmothers. All of a sudden you're too good to play with a horse."

"We don't care," stated Mountain Malone. "Either that horse goes or *we* go!"

Casey Balloo turned to Arch Crabwheat for support. "The team's leaving tomorrow for Houston," said Crabwheat. "It wouldn't hurt for Oscar to stay home."

"Fine help you are," snapped Casey. "You got me into this." Finally he agreed that the

Goats would travel to Houston without the horse.

After the team left the clubhouse, Casey remained with his press secretary. "Archibald, I was against bringing Oscar up here. But the team plays better with him in center field. I can't explain why."

"Maybe they get so mad they try harder," suggested Crabwheat.

Casey stroked his chin. "I always insisted some of these guys had talent. Maybe all we needed to do was stir them up."

Later Arch Crabwheat called Kevin to explain why Oscar couldn't make the trip. "He won't fit on the airplane," explained the press secretary.

Nevertheless, Kevin appeared at the airport the following day to wave good-bye to the team. The players filed past him sullenly without saying a word. If Kevin noticed, he said nothing.

Lefty Oliver also had come to the airport. When he saw Kevin, he started to leave, but he couldn't move very fast on his crutches. "Why don't you have dinner with us tonight?" asked Kevin.

Lefty looked away. "I don't know," he said. He still didn't like the idea of a horse replacing him in center field.

Kevin's grandmother stood nearby. "We'll be

glad to have you, Mr. Oliver," she said. "I'll bake an apple pie."

Lefty might not like horses, but he sure liked apple pie. He finally agreed to come.

That night Lefty Oliver arrived for dinner wearing his best tweed suit, a polka-dot tie, and a bright red sock over his cast. He said little at first. But when Kevin's grandmother presented him with an extra large slice of apple pie, his face lit up with a smile. "Sure was good pie," he said after finishing his third piece.

"We have to hurry," said Kevin, grabbing a portable radio. "The game starts real soon."

"Where are we going?" asked Lefty.

"To the livery stable to see Oscar," announced Kevin. "He'll want to listen to the game too."

After three pieces of apple pie, how could Lefty Oliver say no?

At the livery stable, Oscar greeted Kevin and Lefty with a loud snort. Lefty gave the horse a weak smile and plopped down as far away as possible.

"Come on, Goats!" Kevin shouted as the game began. Oscar whinnied. That was the only way he could cheer.

For seven innings the lead seesawed back and forth between the Goats and the Houston Steers. Then the other team scored four runs. They finally won 7 to 4.

"Gosh, we should have won," said Kevin.

"Well, guess I'll get going," said Lefty. He had moved closer to the radio—and Oscar—during the game.

"You'll be back tomorrow, won't you?" asked Kevin.

Lefty tried to protest, but the following night he appeared at the livery stable once more. The Goats fell three runs behind by the second inning and lost 10 to 2.

Lefty smacked the ground with his crutch. "We're playing as poorly as before your horse joined the team," He was leaning against Oscar's stall when he said it.

On the third night the team had even less luck. The Goats' batters hit weak grounders or struck out. In the field they made error after error. "At least get a hit," pleaded Lefty as the Goats came to bat in the ninth inning. But all three batters struck out. Houston defeated the Goats 17 to 0. Their pitcher didn't allow a single batter to reach first base.

"If Oscar had been there," complained Kevin, "I bet he could have at least gotten a base on balls."

Lefty nodded his head. He stroked the horse on the nose. "You know, Oscar," said Lefty, "for a horse you're not a bad Goat after all."

Lefty and Oscar left the livery stable. They

didn't notice two men seated in a pink sports car across the street.

"So this is where they keep the horse," said Crooknose Jake.

"What do you plan?" asked Louie the Skunk.

"Nothing," Jake replied. "At least for the present."

chapter 8

The Goats returned to play a game at home the next day. When they ran onto the field for the first inning, Oscar trotted with them. He resumed his place in center field. "Hooray, Oscar," chanted the fans. "Hooray, Oscar!"

But the Goats' players didn't appear to be so happy. Fireball Smith walked to the mound seething with anger. Tubby Swenton joined him. They both stared out toward center field.

"All the crowd cares about is that doggone hoss," said Fireball.

"Lose a few games with him playing and see how they like him," grumbled Tubby. He turned to take his place behind the plate.

Fireball Smith spent several seconds more scowling at the horse in center field. "Play ball!" shouted the umpire.

The pitcher turned and directed his anger at the batter. *Zwoooosh!* He fired the baseball fast and straight down the middle. The batter barely had time to blink at it. *Thuunk!* The ball struck Tubby Swenton's mitt so hard the surprised catcher fell backward onto his back.

"Stee-rike one," called the umpire.

Swenton picked himself up from the dust and threw the ball back to his pitcher. "Way to throw, Fireball," he called. "Show them who's the best pitcher in baseball!"

And for nine innings Fireball Smith did just that. When he walked off the mound after facing the last batter, he had pitched a no-hitter. That made two no-hitters in a row the Goats had played in. This one they won. The crowd leaped to its feet to cheer Fireball Smith. His teammates ran to pat him on the back.

"Those cheers are for you, Fireball!" shouted Casey as the pitcher reached the dugout.

"Yeah, I guess they are," said Fireball, a grin spreading across his face. Not a single ball had been hit to center field for Oscar to catch.

Phil Furlong was the first reporter to reach him. "When did you begin to think you had a no-hitter?" he asked.

Fireball Smith looked up at the reporter. "Never thought of it," he explained. "All I could think about during the game was that doggone hoss in center field."

"So Oscar helped you win the ball game," suggested Furlong.

"Now I didn't say that!" snapped Fireball. But this caused him to think.

Later, after he had showered and all the reporters had left the club house, the pitcher turned to Lefty Oliver. "You know, Furlong was right. I got so plumb mad about Casey playing that hoss in center field I forgot to worry about my control."

"Oscar's a good fellow," said Lefty. "You ought to get to know him."

"If I can pitch like this every game," said Fireball, "maybe I will."

The Goats swept their three-game series with the Los Angeles Mules. Then the Atlanta Eagles came to town. The Goats beat them four straight. In each game Oscar played without an error in center field.

"I'm starting to like that horse," Spider Switchstick admitted to Mountain Malone after the last victory.

"Oh, man, don't tell me that," grimaced Malone.

"When Oscar plays, we win," explained Switchstick. "Maybe he brings us luck. You know how some players are about luck. If they get in a winning streak, they try to continue it. They do the same things. They won't even change their socks. They're afraid to break the spell."

"Dirty socks is one thing," snapped the big first baseman. "A horse in center field is another."

Oscar remained in center field and the Goats continued to win. But many of the players still resented him. The fans, however, loved their horse. Attendance at the park doubled. *Time* magazine carried Oscar's picture on its cover. Oscar bubble-gum cards traded even for ten cards of any other players. Girls tried to grasp pieces of his tail. Banquet chairmen wanted Oscar to give an after-dinner whinny.

Sponsors clamored for Oscar to endorse their products. One sponsor wanted Oscar to endorse a laundry soap and appear on TV carrying a knight in white armor on his back.

"I understand some of the players dislike Oscar," Phil Furlong said to Casey Balloo one day. "Is there any truth to that?"

Casey gave the reporter a fatherly smile. "They won't resent him after they win the pennant."

"You must be joking," said Furlong. "The Goats have never finished higher than tenth before."

"There's a first time for everything," said Casey and walked away.

Furlong strolled over to where Kevin stood

stacking bats. "Casey tells me he plans to win the pennant with your horse," said the reporter.

Kevin thought for a while. "Well," he finally said, "Oscar's never played on a losing team before."

Furlong laughed. "That's what your horse is: a winner. He's such a winner that he's even turned a bunch of losers like the Goats into winners."

Meanwhile Crooknose Jake and Louie the Skunk watched. "There's no money to be made here," growled Louie. "The way the Goats are playing with that horse in center field, nobody will bet against them."

"Suppose," suggested Jake, "some day Oscar fails to show up."

Louie looked surprised. "You've got a plan, Jake. Tell me about it."

"No plan yet," said his partner. "Just thinking out loud." The gambler gave an evil cackle.

That day the Goats played the Cincinnati Foxes. The Foxes' manager named Gorilla Brady as his starting pitcher. Brady was a man both hated and feared by players on the other teams. Anyone who hit a home run off Brady could expect to have the ball thrown at his head the next time he came to bat.

Brady stood talking to his catcher before the start of the game. "The Goats depend on that horse to win," growled Brady. "I think I'll pop him with an inside pitch."

"Why worry about that horse?" asked the catcher. "He doesn't hit."

"I want them to know who's boss," snarled Gorilla Brady.

For six innings Gorilla Brady and Fireball Smith pitched scoreless ball. Then, at the start of the seventh, the Foxes punched across two quick runs on three hits and an error by Mountain Malone. Two men stood on second and third with Brady himself at bat.

Bam! Brady smacked the first pitch into right center field. It looked like a sure hit. The base runners headed toward home.

Standing near the batting circle, Kevin shouted: "Run, Oscar, run!"

At the crack of the bat, Oscar moved like a race horse. As the ball sank, Oscar darted toward it. The crowd gasped. He made the catch.

"Second! Second!" shouted Kevin.

The Foxes' runner from second base halted almost at third. He scrambled to get back, but Oscar galloped toward the infield. Just as the Foxes' runner started his slide, Oscar thundered across the base to complete the double play.

"That did it!" snorted Gorilla Brady. "That horse will pay!"

Brady strode to the mound, anger burning his

face. The first batter to face him was Oscar. The pitcher shook off one sign after another from his catcher. Finally he nodded and threw.

Zooom! The pitch came in hard and fast and aimed directly at Oscar's head. Oscar dodged, dropping his bat as he did. On the mound, Gorilla Brady sported an evil smile. In the home-team dugout, the Goats' players suddenly tensed. The fans booed.

"Golly, he's trying to hit Oscar," said Kevin.

"The pitch probably just got away," mumbled Lefty Oliver. But with Gorilla Brady on the mound, he didn't believe it.

Brady wound up and threw again. *Zooom!* This time the pitch was thrown farther inside. Oscar jumped backward so fast that he stumbled and fell over onto his back. A gasp of horror rose from the crowd.

In an instant the Goats' players jumped to the edge of the dugout, as though ready to charge to the mound. But Oscar was unhurt. He rose to his feet and picked the bat up in his teeth once more.

"Look at that horse," said Tubby Swenton, "he's got guts."

"Yeah," Spider Switchstick agreed.

Mountain Malone said nothing. But his eyes burned with an angry fire.

On the mound, Gorilla Brady stood laughing

at the downed horse and the Goats' players. Having made his point, he threw three strikes past Oscar on the next three pitches. Oscar glumly trotted away from the plate.

"Gosh," sighed Kevin.

"Give me my bat," Mountain Malone growled at Kevin. The ground shook as he stroke toward the mound. The big first baseman dug his spikes into the dirt. "Pitch that ball, Gorilla," he shouted. "Just pitch it!" The pitch came curving across the outside corner.

Mountain Malone's shoulders exploded with power. *Bang!* The baseball rocketed straight toward the pitcher's mound. Gorilla Brady barely had time to get his mitt in front of him in self-defense. The ball bounced off it and out into right field. Brady went down in a heap on the mound.

Mountain Malone stood on first base laughing at the fallen pitcher. "Gorilla, if you're going to dish it out, you'd better learn to take it!"

The next seven batters all hit safely, causing Gorilla Brady to exit for another pitcher. The Goats won the game 6 to 2.

After the team had showered, Kevin spoke with Mountain Malone. "I thought you didn't like Oscar, Mr. Malone."

"What do you mean, not like Oscar?" roared the big first baseman. "He's *my man!*"

"But Oscar's a horse," said Kevin.

"He may be a horse, but he's still *my man,*" Malone replied. "And nobody throws at my man without facing *me!*"

From that day, Oscar became a full-fledged Goat. By early September, his team clinched its first National League pennant.

chapter 9

The entire country awaited the opening game of the World Series. The New York Bombers won the American League pennant. They would face the Goats in the seven-game series.

"You'll be playing against your old team," Phil Furlong said to Casey. "Does that make you want to win even more?"

"I just want to win," replied Casey blandly. "It doesn't matter who we play." But secretly he wanted to beat the Bombers so badly he could almost taste it. He wanted to crush them—in four games, if possible. It would be a great note on which to end a baseball career.

The day before the game, Kevin's father and mother arrived from Florida. They stayed with him at his grandmother's house, as did several uncles and cousins. The phone rang constantly with requests for tickets. A mounted policeman called one night.

"I don't want the seat for myself," he pleaded. "It's for my horse."

"Gosh, we're all out of tickets," Kevin told him. "I guess your horse will have to watch the game on television."

The first day of the Series, a large group of fans stood near the door where the teams entered. As each member of the New York Goats arrived, the crowd cheered. They thrust programs into the players' hands, begging for autographs. Then a cry went up: "Here comes Oscar!"

A car pulling a trailer stopped at the curb. Lefty Oliver and Kevin got out. Lefty had the cast off his leg now. The two let Oscar out of the trailer. "Good luck today, Oscar," cried the fans. "Hit one for me."

Several reporters awaited them near the stadium door. "How did Oscar sleep?" Phil Furlong of the *Bugle* asked Kevin.

"Quite well, thanks," Kevin replied.

"What did he have for breakfast?" another reporter asked Kevin.

"A big bagful of oats," replied Kevin. The reporters wrote rapidly in their notebooks.

Kevin and Oscar went inside, unaware that Crooknose Jake and Louie the Skunk watched.

"There's a lot of money riding on the Goats," commented Louie.

"I'm aware of that," said Jake.

"We could hijack the horse's trailer," suggested Louie. "With Oscar out of the line-up, the Goats would lose. We could make a fortune."

"You fool," sneered Jake. "Hijack the trailer here? In front of all these police? Do you think I'm stupid?"

"I just——" began Louie.

"What do you think I've been plotting all these months?" said Jake. "Come here and I'll tell you my plans." He motioned for Louie to follow. The two men vanished into the crowd.

The game began. For five innings neither the Bombers nor the Goats could score. Then in inning six, the Bombers' lead-off batter sliced a grounder between short and third for a base hit.

The next batter dumped a bunt to the right of the pitcher's mound. Fireball Smith came off the mound fast and pounced on the slowly rolling ball. He turned and threw to second, hoping to get the lead runner.

But the throw was late. The Bombers' base runner slid under it, safe. Runners stood on first and second with nobody out.

Fireball Smith pounded his fist into his mitt and his face turned red. He threw four balls to the next batter, the last one sailing so high that

Tubby Swenton had to jump to keep it from going to the screen. Casey Balloo strode out to the pitcher's mound. "Settle down, Fireball," he said.

"Sorry, Casey," said the pitcher.

Casey nodded and returned to the dugout. "Come on, Fireball, put it across the plate," shouted Kevin. And Fireball did. He threw two quick strikes past the next batter. His next pitch barely missed the outside corner.

Swenton signaled for a curve tight around the knees. Fireball shook him off. He waited for another sign, then went into a quick, half wind-up. He aimed his fast ball low, but it slipped off his fingers an instant too early. The pitch came straight down the center. The batter was waiting.

Slam! The ball arched toward the right center-field wall. The crowd gasped. A home run would mean four runs. Even Oscar couldn't defend against a home run—or could he?

The instant the ball left the bat, Oscar started to run. He sprinted onto the warning track in front of the outfield wall. As the baseball started to fall, he crouched ready to spring. At the last second, he propelled himself upward with his powerful rear legs. He stretched his neck as long as he could.

"Oscar caught it!" shouted Kevin. "He caught it!" And sixty thousand fans sank limply back into their seats. One base runner tagged up and scored from third, but the next batter hit into a double play. The Bombers led 1 to 0.

Mountain Malone tied the game in the sixth with a home run. Then, in the eighth inning, two singles and an infield error loaded the bases for the Goats. The fans clapped their hands and stomped their feet. Spider Switchstick reached for a bat in the rack.

"Wish me luck, Oscar," he said, patting the horse on the nose. Oscar whinnied cheerfully at him.

The Bombers' manager waved his ace relief pitcher in from the bull pen. "Pitch him over the plate," instructed the manager. "Switchstick's learned to field, but he still can't hit."

If the pitcher had done what his manager told him, the Bombers might have won. But he threw six pitches—four of them balls. Switchstick walked, forcing in a run. The Goats won 2 to 1 and led the Series by one game.

Up in the press box, some of the out-of-town reporters marveled at the Goats' victory. "Did you see what Switchstick did?" said one.

"What did he do?" asked Phil Furlong.

"Just before he got that base on balls, he patted Oscar on the nose," said the first reporter. "It's almost as though that horse brings the Goats good luck."

"You don't say," said Furlong. He knew it

was more than that. Oscar had simply awakened in the Goats a desire to win.

In the second game, the Goats scored three runs in the second inning. They added two more each in the fourth and fifth, to coast to a 7 to 3 victory over the Bombers. Two days later in Bombers Stadium, the Goats won again, 9 to 4, to move within one game of the world championship.

"I don't know what the Goats would do without that horse," commented one reporter after the game.

"I know what they would do," said Phil Furlong.

"What's that?"

"They would lose."

And outside the ball park, two gamblers plotted exactly that. They waited in their pink sports car until Lefty and Kevin appeared with Oscar. Then they followed the car and the trailer to the livery stable. Driving past, they parked around the next corner.

"Everything is ready," said Louie.

"Then tomorrow we strike," hissed Crooknose Jake.

chapter 10

Many sports writers expected the Goats to win the next game too and thus end the World Series. They gave the Bombers little chance. "One thing is certain," wrote Phil Furlong on the day of the fourth game. "The Bombers are one horse short of having a well-rounded ball club."

At nine that morning, Lefty Oliver arrived at Kevin's grandmother's house. As usual, he would drive Kevin to the livery stable. They would pick up Oscar and drive to the ball park. Kevin finished his breakfast and they started for the car. "Good luck," said Kevin's father.

"We'll see you after the game," his mother said.

Kevin and Lefty climbed into the car. They were being watched. Louie the Skunk stood across the street, hidden in a doorway. After the two drove away, Louie moved quickly to a phone booth at the end of the block. He dialed a number.

"It's Louie," the gambler barked into the phone. "They're on the way." Then he hung up.

Lefty drove along the expressway. The day was sunny and bright. Arriving at the stable, Lefty drove the car around to the rear. Kevin went inside to get Oscar. Lefty started to attach the horse trailer to his car. The attendant came out to help him.

"Going to win today?" asked the attendant.

"With Oscar, we can't lose," smiled Lefty.

Kevin led Oscar from his stall and into the trailer. He snapped the latch on the trailer gate. At that moment a telephone sounded inside the stable office. "I'll have to answer that," said the attendant.

Kevin and Lefty climbed into the car. Lefty started the engine. Before they could move, however, the attendant appeared again in the yard.

"The phone call's for you, Mr. Oliver," announced the attendant. "They said it was urgent."

Leaving the enging running, Lefty climbed out of the car. He walked to the office with the attendant. Kevin remained in the car. A few seconds later, the door next to the driver's seat opened again.

Kevin looked up, expecting to see Lefty. Instead he saw a gun pointed at his throat.

"Don't say a word," snarled Crooknose Jake. He climbed inside. With him at the wheel, the car leaped forward. In the trailer, Oscar whinnied in surprise. Several hundred yards down the road, Jake stopped the car and shoved the gun in Kevin's ribs.

"Get out!" spat the gambler. "We want the horse, not you."

Kevin stood on the sidewalk as car and trailer sped out of sight around the corner. For several seconds, Kevin couldn't move. Then he ran back toward the stable.

Lefty and the attendant stood in the stable yard with puzzled looks on their faces. "Where's Oscar?" asked Lefty.

Kevin quickly told him about the man with the gun. "Who was on the telephone?" he asked Lefty.

"Nobody. He hung up as soon as I answered. Whoever called was a friend of the man with the gun. It's a plot against Oscar."

"He's been kidnaped," said the attendant.

"But why kidnap Oscar?" asked Kevin.

Lefty paused and thought. "Because someone wants us to lose the World Series."

"Could it be somebody from the Bombers?"

"No," explained Lefty. "They wouldn't cheat to win. But maybe someone who had money on the game. Gamblers, maybe. They want us to lose so they can collect their bets."

"But what can we do?" asked Kevin.

"Call the police and——" began Lefty.

"And what?"

"And pray nothing happens to Oscar."

Kevin and Lefty started to walk toward the office. At the doorway, Kevin paused as though remembering something. "That man with the gun," he said, "somehow I feel I've seen him before."

"Try and remember," said Lefty. "We'll need every clue we can get." They went inside to call the police.

At that instant, Crooknose Jake sped across town with the stolen automobile. In the trailer behind, Oscar whinnied for help. But no one could hear over the roar of the motor.

Two miles from the stable, Jake glanced in the rear mirror. A pink sports car had fallen in line behind him. Inside was Louie the Skunk. He had placed the call that brought Lefty to the phone and allowed Jake to act.

"Ha ha," crackled Crooknose Jake. "Without Oscar, the Goats will lose the World Series."

The gambler continued to laugh. The two desperate villains and one frightened horse disappeared down the highway.

chapter II

"OSCAR HORSE-NAPED," shouted the headline in the New York *Bugle*. "FAMOUS BASEBALL HORSE TAKEN FROM STABLE."

Phil Furlong wrote: "Oscar, star center fielder for the New York Goats, vanished from his stable yesterday morning. He was leaving to play in the fourth game of the World Series against the New York Bombers. Without their horse in center field, the dispirited Goats lost 7 to 2."

The story continued: "Police searching the New York area have failed to uncover any clues. Goats' manager Casey Balloo said: 'I hope nothing has happened to Oscar. We'll have to go out and win without him.' "

In a secluded and run-down house on Long

Island, not far from Goats Stadium, Crooknose Jake read the story and laughed: "Win without that horse? Never happen. The Goats will lose the World Series and we'll win a fortune. And what's best, we'll get revenge against Casey Balloo."

He threw the paper onto a table. Louie the Skunk began to look at it.

"What are you doing?" snorted Jake. "You can't read."

"I like to look at the pictures," explained Louie.

Jake walked to the window and gazed at the stable in back. They had locked Oscar within. Trees completely surrounded the area. A wealthy horsebreeder, who once raced his horses at a race track a mile down the road, formerly owned the house and stable. When he died, the property fell into disrepair. It had been deserted for years when Crooknose Jake discovered the place.

"They'll never find us here," he boasted to his partner.

"What if they find the stolen car and trailer?" asked Louie.

"We left them one hundred miles away down in New Jersey," answered Jake. "Suppose the police do find them. They'll never trace us here almost in the Goats' back yard. Meanwhile, we'll stay hidden and watch the Bombers win."

Jake glanced at his watch. "Time for the game," he announced. Louie switched on the TV set. It flickered grayish-blue, then a picture of Bombers Stadium on the other side of town appeared. Jake and Louie watched as neither team scored in the early innings. Then in the fourth inning, the powerful Bombers exploded for three runs. The final score of the game: Bombers 8, Goats 1.

Crooknose Jake switched off the set. "They'll never win without their horse!" he shouted in triumph.

On the morning of the sixth game, Oscar had not been found. The team filed into the club house a dejected group. "We haven't given up yet," Casey Balloo told the newsmen. But inside he knew the team's spirit had died.

Kevin stopped Phil Furlong on the way to the field. "Is there any hope?" he asked the reporter.

"We have a man at the police station," Furlong replied. "As soon as anything breaks, he'll call me."

In the sixth game, the Goats could manage only four hits. The Bombers beat them 11 to 0.

That tied the teams at three games each. One more win by either club would end the World

Series. But the police still had found no trace of Oscar.

"It looks bad," Arch Crabwheat admitted to Casey.

At seven o'clock on the morning of the seventh game, the telephone rang in Kevin's grandmother's house. Lefty Oliver was calling. Kevin ran to the phone still in his pajamas. "Have they found Oscar?" he asked.

"No," came Lefty's voice, "but Phil Furlong is here. His office called to say the police found my car and the trailer. We'll pick you up in fifteen minutes."

Kevin had time to finish his breakfast. Then he heard a car honk. Phil Furlong was driving. Lefty sat in the right seat. "Hop in," said Lefty.

Lefty explained that the New Jersey state police found the car and trailer abandoned on a dirt road. They drove for what seemed a long time before reaching the road. A single policeman stood on guard. "That's Oscar's trailer, all right," said Kevin. "But where is Oscar?"

"We're searching the area," explained the policeman. "We think your horse may be hidden somewhere nearby."

"Any clues?" asked Kevin.

"Only one," said the policeman. "A farmer down the road remembers seeing a pink sports car near here several days ago. It was about the same time this trailer was dumped."

"A pink sports car——" began Kevin.

"The farmer had never seen such a flashy car before. It must have been going ninety miles per hour down the road."

"A pink sports car!" said Kevin, snapping his fingers. It all came clear to him now. He remembered where he had seen the man who had pointed the gun at him. The day the Goats played in Chatahatchee, Florida, two men drove past their house in a pink sports car. They had asked how to get to the stadium.

When Kevin told the others, Lefty said: "Find that car and we'll find Oscar."

The policeman asked Lefty to sign for the car and trailer, then he drove off. Phil Furlong meanwhile bent low to examine the trailer wheels.

"What are you looking for?" asked Kevin.

"Mud," said the reporter. Reaching into his pocket, he pulled out a jackknife. Furlong scraped some reddish-looking mud from one wheel. He compared it to the mud on the road. The mud on the road was yellowish-brown.

"Why, the mud's not the same," said Kevin.

"I'll bet wherever we find mud like that we'll find Oscar," said Lefty. Then he sighed. "But that's a big wherever."

Furlong crumbled the mud in his hand. "Before I covered baseball, I covered the races. I remember one race track that had thick mud in the parking lot. I often had to scrape it off my shoes."

"And the mud was this color?" asked Kevin.

The reporter nodded.

"Gamblers hang out around race tracks," said Lefty. "And gamblers would profit most if the Goats lost."

"What are we waiting for?" shouted Kevin. He looked at his watch. It was almost game time.

He and Lefty dashed for their car. They sped off down the road with Furlong following behind. By the time they reached the race track, the Goats were already losing 2 to 0 in the fourth inning. "Even if we do find Oscar, it may be too late," groaned Kevin. They drove around the outside of the track to the stable area.

"Be careful where you park the car," Kevin warned Lefty. "It's pretty muddy back here."

A man approached. "Can I help you?" he asked.

"We're looking for a horse," said Kevin.

The man laughed. "Well, we've got plenty of them here," he said and waved his hand toward a large pasture. Several dozen horses behind a fence stood grazing the grass.

"We're trying to find Oscar, the center fielder for the Goats," Kevin explained. "He's been kidnaped. We think he may be held nearby."

"Say, I know who you are," said the man.

"You're Kevin Darling." Kevin nodded his head.

"The police found Oscar's trailer this morning," said Lefty Oliver. "It had mud on the wheels like this."

The man examined the red mud in Lefty's hand. "That's from here, all right," he said. "No other valley in five hundred miles has mud of that kind. But I haven't seen your horse. Feel free to look around."

"Have you seen anyone around here driving a pink sports car?" asked Phil Furlong.

The man's jaw dropped. "That sounds like Crooknose Jake, the gambler," he said. "We barred him from this race track two years ago for fixing a race. Strange that you should mention him. I saw Jake in the village only two days ago."

"Where is he now?" asked Kevin.

The man walked to the end of the fence and pointed up a long hill. "I saw him driving that way," he said. "There's nothing up there but an old, deserted house and stable. Used to belong to a horse breeder."

Lefty and Furlong looked quickly at each other, then ran for the car. "Thanks," said Kevin, and he sprinted after them.

Furlong drove up the road to near the deserted house, then pulled to one side. "They'll see us if we come by car," he said. "Let's circle in from the woods."

Lefty and Furlong crossed through a ditch with Kevin behind them. They moved stealthily through a forest area. A barbed-wire fence blocked their path.

First Lefty, then Furlong, slid under the fence. Kevin dropped on the ground to follow. He moved forward on his belly when suddenly he felt the barbed wire catch his coat. The two men glanced around to see what delayed him. Kevin waved them on. It took him a few seconds to free his coat. By then his friends had vanished into the trees.

Kevin rose and started after them. He had gone fifty feet when a voice shouted: "All right, don't move. I see you!"

Kevin froze in his tracks. Through the trees he saw a man move from behind a shed. He carried a shotgun. But the gun wasn't pointed at him. The man pointed it at Lefty and Furlong, who stood at the edge of a clearing.

Kevin realized he hadn't yet been seen. Slowly he moved behind a large oak tree. With the tree between him and the man with the shotgun, he slid quietly to the ground. Finally he rolled over underneath some thick bushes.

"I've caught somebody out here!" the man shouted.

Kevin lifted his head. He could see partly into the clearing where his friends had been caught. At that moment, a second man came out of the farmhouse. He had a crooked nose.

Kevin gasped. It was the same man who had pulled the gun on him and kidnaped Oscar. They had come to the right place.

"I recognize these two," said Crooknose Jake. "Lefty Oliver, former center fielder for the New York Goats, and Phil Furlong, star reporter of the New York *Bugle*."

"You rats," muttered Lefty.

"You might like to know," cackled the gangster, "that it's the sixth inning now. The Goats are losing 3 to 0. It's all over for them." Then he added: "And it's also all over for *you!*"

Kevin heard a horse's whinny. It came from the nearby stable. He recognized the whinny as belonging to Oscar.

"That's your friend," Crooknose Jake snarled. "Maybe you'd like to join him." Kevin saw Jake motion to Louie the Skunk. "Take them inside and tie them up."

"Okay, boss," said Louie. He prodded the two with the barrel of his shotgun.

Kevin wanted to get up and run, or scream. He finally decided to lie still. The two crooks pushed Lefty and Furlong into the stable. A few minutes later they appeared again in the yard.

Crooknose Jake handed Louie a pair of car

keys. "I found these keys in Furlong's pocket. They probably left their car on the highway. Go find it and bring it here."

"Okay, boss," said Louie.

He took the keys from the other man. Then to Kevin's horror, he began walking through the woods toward him.

Kevin buried his face under the bushes. He felt the ground vibrate as the man approached. Soon the footsteps had almost reached him.

Kevin wanted to shout: "Don't shoot! Don't shoot!" But he kept quiet.

The footsteps soon moved away. Kevin breathed easily again when he realized he hadn't been seen. He heard the whine of an automobile starter, then Louie drove the car into the yard. After parking it, he entered the house.

The yard fell silent except for an occasional whinny from Oscar. Kevin realized that unless he could bring help, the gamblers would escape. And who knew what they might do to his friends before leaving?

After what seemed like hours, Kevin rolled out from under the bush that hid him. He slid on his belly back under the barbed-wire fence. He continued to crawl on his hands and knees until he knew for certain the gamblers could no longer see or hear him.

Even if we do free Oscar, thought Kevin, it

will be too late for the Goats. Without Oscar, they'll lose the World Series. It would take a miracle to save them now.

Kevin suddenly felt something on his face. He held out his palm and several drops of water fell onto it.

Rain!

Kevin rose to his feet and started to run.

chapter 12

It seemed to Kevin that he never would find the highway again. He tripped several times in his flight from the gamblers. Tree branches slapped at his face. His lungs burned from the effort of escaping. Finally he stumbled into the open.

He looked down the highway toward the race track where they had stopped earlier. Would there be time to reach it and call the police? His friends' lives might depend on his speed. He started to run down the road.

So intent was Kevin on his goal that he failed to hear a truck approach from behind. Suddenly it was upon him. Its brakes screeched. Kevin jumped off the road in fright. Had the gamblers caught him?

The driver of the truck rolled down his window. "You're going to get hit running down the road like that," he shouted. "Want a ride?"

Kevin wiped the rain from his forehead. It was only a farmer trying to be friendly. "Thanks," said Kevin, and climbed inside. "I'm going to the race track."

The truck started up. "If you're in such a hurry, you'd better borrow one of their horses," said the farmer.

Kevin smiled weakly. The farmer was listening to the baseball game on the truck radio. "What inning is it?" asked Kevin.

"Eighth," the farmer replied. "Bombers still winning."

When the farmer let him out of the truck, Kevin ran back to the stable area. The horses still grazed in the pasture nearby. No one else was in sight. Kevin located the office and found the stable owner watching the baseball game on television.

"Say, what happened to you?" the man asked as Kevin ran in the door.

Kevin looked down at his clothes. He had torn his trousers and his leg bled from a fall. He was wet from the rain. But he had no time to worry about minor problems. "We found Oscar," he announced.

"I'll call the police," said the man.

Kevin held up his hand to stop him. "Wait,"

he said. Kevin fixed his gaze on the television set. Rain had delayed the start of the ninth inning. The screen showed the stadium workers rolling a large canvas over the infield.

"Before you call the police," said Kevin, "first call the Goats!"

Back at the baseball park, the Goats' team trudged from the field and slumped down on stools in front of their lockers. No one spoke. When the game began again, they had one inning to turn defeat into victory. But it was clear from their faces that no one believed they could do it. The rain only delayed the loss.

"Oh man," said Mountain Malone. "My soul hurts."

Casey walked to the center of the room. "All right, boys," he began. "Don't give up yet."

Tubby Swenton shook his head. "It's no use, Casey," he murmured. "Without Oscar, it's no use."

Casey started to speak, but words failed him. At that moment, Arch Crabwheat ran into the room. "The phone, Casey," shouted the press secretary. "It's important!"

Casey reached for the phone on the wall. His face lit up. "What?" he said. "What?"

"What's up, Case?" asked Fireball Smith.

Casey hung up the phone. "That was Kevin. They've found Oscar."

Fireball Smith jumped from his stool. "Where?"

"Up near the race track," said Casey. "Oscar's being held by some gamblers. Kevin's called the police."

"Who needs police?" roared Mountain Malone, grabbing a bat from the rack. "Let's go get him ourselves!"

"But we've got a game to finish," began Casey. Nobody heard him.

Malone ran for the door. With a cheer, the other Goats raced after him. Each one paused long enough to select a bat.

Casey stood dumfounded for a moment. "Wait for me," he shouted. "Wait for me!"

The Goats stopped outside the stadium as though uncertain what to do next. Then they spotted a large yellow bus parked by the curb. A large sign on it read: "Chartered."

The Goats scrambled onto the bus. The driver looked up from the newspaper he had been reading in surprise. He couldn't understand why several dozen men wearing baseball uniforms and carrying bats suddenly had invaded his bus.

"Hey, you can't use this bus," he said. "It's chartered by the Glen Ridge Kiwanis Club."

"The Glen Ridge Kiwanis Club ain't going nowhere until we come back and finish the game," said Fireball Smith. He waved his bat over the driver's head. "Drive us to the race track."

The bus lurched away from the curb just as Casey Balloo appeared on the sidewalk. "Hey, wait for me!" shouted Casey, but it was too late.

Casey stood for several seconds watching the retreating bus. "Well, I'll be darned," he finally said. "Here I am in the middle of a World Series game without a team."

Kevin stood outside the race-track office looking anxiously toward the road. It seemed like hours since he had telephoned for help. Unless help arrived soon, who knew what might happen to his friends?

At that moment he heard the roar of an automobile engine. "It must be the police," Kevin said to himself.

But it wasn't the police. Instead a large, yellow bus rounded the corner and slid to a halt in the muddy parking lot. Baseball players carrying bats started spilling out the door.

"Where's Oscar?" asked Mountain Malone.

"He's being held in a farmhouse up the road," explained Kevin.

"Get back in the bus," shouted Fireball Smith. Everyone jumped back into their seats. Fireball turned to the driver. "Up the road. Quick!"

The driver rammed the gear-shift lever forward and goosed the engine. The bus failed to move. Its wheels spun in the mud. The driver tried reverse, but nothing happened.

"We're stuck in the mud," sighed the bus driver.

The Goats piled out of the bus, still carrying their bats. They stood in the rain and looked at the rear wheels of the bus sunk deep in the mud.

"It'll take us all day to push the bus out of here," moaned Tubby Swenton.

Fireball Smith, however, looked to where the race-track horses stood grazing in the pasture. "Doggone! I'm not going to wait for the bus," he shouted.

Smith ran for the pasture. He took the fence in one jump and caught the nearest horse. "Giddyap, hoss. Let's go rescue Oscar!"

With a shout, each of the other Goats ran for the pasture and selected a horse. The stable owner moved to open the gate.

"God bless you," he cried, and the horses, each carrying a baseball player, stampeded out, headed up the road.

"The cavalry is coming!" shouted Mountain Malone, swinging a bat high over his head. "The cavalry is coming!"

"Come back. Come back!" yelled the bus driver. "What will the Glen Ridge Kiwanis say?"

chapter 13

Back at the farmhouse, Crooknose Jake and Louie the Skunk threw a pair of suitcases into the trunk of their sports car. "We'd better hurry," said Jake. "If those two found us, others may be close behind."

"What about the horse?" asked Louie.

"I'll see about him right now," said Jake. He flicked an ash from his cigar and headed for the stable.

Lefty Oliver and Phil Furlong lay on the floor of the stable, their hands and legs bound by ropes. Oscar stood helpless in a nearby stall.

Jake walked over to Oscar and attempted to pat the horse. But the horse backed away. The gambler sneered at him. "A great center fielder you turned out to be. One more inning and the

Goats lose the series—and we win a pile of money."

"You'll never get away with this," grumbled Phil Furlong.

"We already have," said the gambler.

"You rat!" said Furlong.

The gambler turned away. "Sorry," he said. "The Rats don't play in the major leagues."

As one last angry gesture, Crooknose Jake threw his cigar at the two bound captives. He walked out the door, locking it behind him.

Furlong and Lefty started to struggle with the ropes holding them. They failed to notice that the cigar thrown by the gambler landed behind them in a pile of hay.

Crooknose Jake returned to the house. A radio on a table was tuned to the baseball game. "The rain seems to be letting up," said the announcer. "Play will resume in a short while. And now a word from our sponsor."

Jake yanked the plug from the wall, silencing the announcer in the middle of a razor blade commercial. He motioned for Louie to take the radio to the car. Crooknose Jake took one last look around the room. Then he went outside.

Louie had the motor running. "I think I hear something," he said, "like thunder."

"Of course, you fool," said Jake. "It's raining." He sat behind the wheel. "Let's get out of here!"

The gambler shoved the sports car in gear. The car roared along the driveway toward the main road. But inside the stable, the thrown cigar had ignited a pile of hay. Flames lapped against one wall.

"This place is on fire," yelled Lefty.

"We've got to get out of here," said Furlong. Though his hands and legs were still bound, he stood. The reporter hopped to the door and threw himself at it.

"It doesn't budge," he said, coughing as his lungs filled with smoke. Oscar began to prance up and down in his stall, whinnying in panic.

Meanwhile, Jake and Louie continued down the driveway. The sound of thunder grew louder. Jake suddenly realized what caused the noise. He slammed on the brakes. "Horses!" he shouted.

"Millions of them!" echoed Louie in fright.

"With baseball players on their backs," said Jake.

"Carrying bats!" screamed Louie.

Mountain Malone and Kevin rode at the front of the pack. "There they are," roared the big first baseman, waving his bat over his head. "Get them!"

The horses thundered toward the halted sports car. Jake quickly spun the car around and raced back toward the house. "There's a back exit!" he snarled. "We've got more horse-power than they do!"

The sports car leaped along the driveway, spraying gravel in its wake. The mounted Goats rumbled relentlessly after it. As Kevin rode past the stable, however, he saw it was on fire. He motioned for Mountain Malone to stop.

"Oscar, Furlong and Lefty are inside," he shouted.

The two jumped to the ground. The rest of the players swept past, intent on pursuing the gamblers.

"We've got to get them out of there," yelled Mountain Malone over the noise of the burning stable.

They approached the stable, but the flames drove them back. Malone shielded his face with his hands, but couldn't get closer than ten feet. The front door was ablaze.

"There must be another entrance," said Kevin. "There has to be!"

He ran around the back, with Malone follow-ing. There, in one corner of the building, was a small doorway. Kevin jiggled the handle "Locked!" he said.

"Stand back," said Malone. He cocked the bat in his hand and swung. *Kuh-bam!* The door flew off its hinges. If it had been a baseball, it would have gone five hundred feet.

Kevin stumbled inside, blinded at first by the heavy smoke. He dropped to his hands and knees to find fresher air and saw Lefty and Furlong lying in the middle of the floor.

"Untie us quickly," Furlong gasped. "This building won't hold much longer."

Kevin and Malone fumbled with the knots. "They're too tight," said the first baseman.

Then Kevin remembered the jackknife used by the reporter to scrape mud from the trailer wheels. "Your knife? Where is it?"

Furlong indicated his left pocket.

With the knife they quickly cut the bonds. Kevin ran to the stall to free Oscar. Oscar rushed out, then began prancing in circles as though not knowing which way to go next.

"Let's get out of here!" shouted Malone.

Kevin started toward the back door, then stopped. Oscar would never fit through it. "We've got to get that front door open," he said.

But flames covered the door. They couldn't get near it.

Mountain Malone ran to a cart standing in the corner.

"Just follow me!" he shouted. He grasped the cart by the handle. Then running straight forward with it ahead of him, he smashed it into the burning door. *Ga-voom!* The door shuddered once and then toppled open.

Oscar didn't wait an instant. He leaped through the opening. Kevin and the others followed. They had hardly gotten out when the walls of the stable started to shudder. Within seconds the building collapsed, sending a shower of sparks into the sky.

Furlong and Lefty fell coughing onto the grass. Kevin turned to Malone. There was still unfinished business. "The gamblers," said Kevin. The two remounted their horses.

While the two had stopped at the burning stable, the rest of the team had galloped off in pursuit of the gamblers. Jake and Louie gunned their sports car toward the farm's back gate.

"In another second, we'll be free," cackled Jake. Suddenly he slammed his foot on the brake. The sports car slid again to a stop.

A fire truck, its roof light flashing red, blocked their retreat. Someone had spotted the smoke and called the fire department.

"Trapped," moaned Louie the Skunk.

"Not yet," snapped Crooknose Jake. He spun the sports car's wheel once more and turned into the open field. The car bounced across the finely sodded grass. "If we can just make the woods, maybe we can escape on foot."

"There they go," shouted Fireball Smith. He turned his horse into the field and the rest of the team turned with him. On the uneven ground, the horses started to gain ground. "They're catching us," whined Louie the Skunk.

Jake whipped the car in a new direction, losing the pursuing baseball players for a moment. Kevin and Mountain Malone meanwhile angled across the field to meet the speeding car.

Malone urged his horse on faster, until he was even with the rear fender of the car. Then he raised his bat over his head and let it fall with a crash. The car's rear window splintered, showering the gamblers inside with glass.

"Watch out!" cried Louie. Jake spun the wheel again, but now the other players on horseback had caught the car. Another bat crashed down on the rear of the car, causing the trunk to spring open.

Crash! Crash! Crash! The car slowed and finally ground to a halt under the rain of bats. "We give up! Don't hurt us!" pleaded the two gamblers inside.

The players lowered their bats. Furlong and Lefty arrived on foot just in time to see the two gamblers stagger out of the battered car with their hands high. The whine of police sirens sounded in the distance.

"It looks like the Rats have lost today," said Furlong. "But maybe so have the Goats."

Kevin held his palm out in front of him. "The rain has stopped," he announced.

Mountain Malone looked at Spider Switchstick, who looked at Tubby Swenton, who looked at Fireball Smith. "Doggone," said Fireball. "I've got to pitch the next inning."

chapter 14

Casey Balloo stared blankly out toward the baseball diamond, his heart heavy in his chest. The end was near. His dream had faded. Victory in the World Series seemed so close, yet he could not grasp it.

The rain had stopped. The grounds crew were rolling the canvas covering off the field. The ninth inning was about to start, with his team losing 3 to 0.

That was Casey's trouble. He didn't have a baseball team.

"Well, where are they?" roared one of the four umpires standing before him.

Casey gave him an innocent-boy smile.

"Where are they?" repeated the umpire. "You just don't go around losing baseball teams. Baseball *games*, yes. Entire baseball *teams*, no! What's the cause of this, Casey?"

"A funny thing happened to me on the way to the baseball park," began the Goats' manager.

"There's nothing funny about this," said the umpire. "Unless you have your team on the field in two minutes, you forfeit the game to the Bombers!"

Casey just groaned.

The fans seated in the left-field bleachers heard it first: a rumbling sound, like thunder, the pounding of horse's hoofs on concrete. The ticket collector at the rear gate looked up to see a herd of horses headed toward him. In front came Oscar, with Kevin on his back. With one graceful leap, Oscar sailed over the turnstile and into the park.

"Watch out," shouted Kevin over his shoulder. "More horses coming!"

Another horse, with Lefty Oliver astride it, cleared the turnstile. Then another and another. In groups of twos and threes the horses leaped into the ball park. Each one carried a member of the Goats' ball club. The final horse carried Phil Furlong across the turnstile. The ticket collector raised his head. "Who's got the tickets?" he screamed.

"Send the bill to Arch Crabwheat," yelled Furlong as his horse followed the others onto the playing field.

The moment that Kevin rode Oscar into left field, the stadium exploded with noise. As the other horses followed, carrying more Goats, the cheers rolled across the playing field like waves on a beach.

A great smile of joy crossed Casey Balloo's face. "Bless the Lord," he said. "The cavalry has arrived."

Kevin dismounted near third base. "Is it too late, Mr. Balloo?" he asked. "Can Oscar play?"

"Oscar can go right into center field," said Casey.

But the Bombers' manager was angry. "Wait a minute," he cried. "Maybe you can get away with one horse in center field, but not half a hundred." He pointed at the herd of horses now clustered around second base. The Goats' players had dismounted.

"Can't they see the game?" Kevin asked the umpire. "Without them, we never would have saved Oscar."

"How about it, Ump?" added Casey. "We can put them behind the bull-pen fence in left field."

The umpire nodded his head. "All right, but get them out of the way fast." The Bombers' manager stormed away.

"It's going to be a pleasure to beat that man," said Casey with a wink.

It took ten minutes to clear the field. Then Oscar trotted out to center field, his baseball cap perched jauntily on his head. The fans in the center-field bleachers stood and cheered him. It was the first half of the ninth inning.

Fireball Smith stalked to the mound, feeling ten feet tall. He threw nine pitches. Each one was a strike.

As the Goats ran from the field to take their turn at bat, Mountain Malone let out a roar: "How sweet it is!"

Casey clapped his hands. "We still need four runs to beat them. Let's get some hits!"

And hit they did. The first batter singled. Then Mountain Malone rapped a double to left field. The other runner took third. The next batter walked.

Spider Switchstick stood at the plate and watched two balls sail by. Then he swung. *Smash!* The ball headed on a straight line between the shortstop and the third baseman. A certain hit.

But the Bombers' third baseman dived for the ball. He trapped the ball between his mitt and the ground and slid across the grass. Rising, he fired the ball to the plate. Out! The catcher rifled the ball to first base in time to catch Switchstick out by a foot. A double play.

Two men were out, but the Goats still had runners on second and third. Tubby Swenton stepped up to the plate, ready to send the ball flying all the way to Russia. At that moment, the Bombers' manager called time.

He walked to the mound and talked to his pitcher. The pitcher nodded. After the manager returned to the dugout, the pitcher lobbed the ball wide of the plate. "Ball one," cried the umpire.

The fans let loose a torrent of boos. After the fourth wide pitch, Tubby Swenton jogged to first base. The bases were loaded, but the next person in the batting order was the center fielder. Oscar had to bat and he hadn't gotten on base all season.

"Oh, that scoundrel," groaned Casey. "He knows I don't have a single pinch hitter left. Even with Oscar, the game is lost."

Casey turned toward his dugout and looked at the half-dozen men remaining. All of them pitchers. Not one could hit the weight of his shower clogs. Suddenly a familiar face floated into view.

"Hi, Casey," said Lefty Oliver.

"Lefty," smiled Casey Balloo. "Lefty Oliver." Lefty hadn't played since Oscar replaced him in center field, but what did that matter? "Good old Lefty Oliver," said Casey.

"Yessir, Mr. Balloo," said Lefty.

"Lefty," pleaded Casey Balloo. "I want you to bat. At least get hit by a pitched ball."

Lefty Oliver had no time to don a uniform. He stripped the suit coat from his back and handed it to the Goats' manager. He loosened his tie. He walked to the bat rack and selected a blunt-tipped model. He polished it lovingly with one hand. Then he rolled up his sleeves and strode to the plate.

The Bombers' pitcher reared back and fired a fast ball that caught the outside corner. "Stee-rike one," shouted the umpire.

Casey, standing in the dugout, covered his eyes with his hands. "I can't look," he moaned.

"Lefty won't let you down," Kevin consoled him.

Again the Bombers' pitcher bent low to get the sign from his catcher. He delivered. *Woosh!* "Stee-rike two," said the umpire.

"Ohhhh," moaned Casey. "Mighty Lefty will strike out."

The next pitch came in and it was a wasted pitch: ball one. Sixty thousand fans in the stands sighed in relief. The pitcher's next delivery came across wide and high: ball two. Sitting in the box seats, Arch Crabwheat rose to his feet and more pleaded than shouted: "Come on, Lefty. Just a single. Keep the rally going!"

The pitcher peered straight ahead, ignoring the runners on first, second, and third. He fired one hard and fast. Lefty started to swing, but didn't break his wrists. *Thump!* The ball snapped into the catcher's mitt. The umpire paused as though afraid to give the call.

"Ball three," he finally said. Casey Balloo almost collapsed in the dugout.

The pitcher stepped forward off the mound and glared at the umpire, as though hoping he might change his mind. The catcher turned to argue, but the umpire raised one hand for silence.

Lefty Oliver stepped out of the batter's box and reached for some dirt. He rubbed the dirt on the handle of the bat. He stretched once. He looked at the center-field scoreboard. It showed the score 3 to 0 against them. The count was three balls and two strikes. There were two out. He glanced at the three runners standing on first, second, and third bases. A long time had passed since last spring when Casey lifted him out of the line-up and put a horse in his place.

Lefty stepped back in the box and knocked the next pitch over the center-field scoreboard.

chapter 15

Casey Balloo leaned back in his lawn chair and sighed with content. He gazed at the rows and rows of orange trees that stretched to the horizon. He owned most of them. With his share of the winning World Series money, he had bought an orange grove.

The Goats won the Series, of course. Lefty's homer with three men on had done it. The score was 4 to 3.

The gamblers were jailed. They would remain in jail a long time. Horse-naping is a serious crime.

Casey had managed his last big league team. He quit while he was on top. Now when he wanted to see a baseball game, he wandered down the road to where the Chatahatchee Alligators played every week end. They had this great outfielder named O'Grady. He also was mayor and led the school band.

Casey heard a whinny from down the road. It was Oscar. Oscar and Kevin often came to visit him. It seemed a shame that the major league owners passed a rule that winter outlawing horses in major league baseball games. They were right, of course. It would change the sport too much.

"Hi there, Mr. Balloo," said Kevin. Oscar neighed a greeting.

"Hi, Kevin," said Casey. "Hi, Oscar."

Kevin dismounted. He had a football tucked under one arm. "What have you been doing?" asked Casey. "Playing football?"

"Well, Mr. Balloo," began Kevin. "Now that Oscar can't play baseball any more, he's getting restless."

"Now wait a minute," said Casey. "I know he can catch baseballs in his mouth, but a football is three times as large."

"Oh, we know that," said Kevin. He turned and fixed his gaze on a pair of palm trees near the road. "How far away are those palm trees?"

Casey turned his head. "Maybe fifty or sixty yards."

"And they're about twenty or twenty-five feet apart," added Kevin. "Right?"

Casey nodded.

"They're about the same distance apart as—"

and here Kevin paused: "football goal posts."

Casey eyed the two trees again. When he turned back to look at Kevin, he saw the boy had dropped to one knee. Kevin held the football against the ground with one finger.

Casey's jaw dropped in disbelief. In that instant Oscar trotted up to the football and kicked it with his right hoof. The football sailed up in the air and passed directly between the two palm trees.

"Now playing in center field," crackles the loudspeaker, "an unknown horse!"

"That's *my* horse," says a stunned Kevin. *"That's Oscar!"*

It's no horselaugh—Oscar's the star player for the New York Goats, a major league team with a mile-long losing streak. But when Oscar's brilliant playing turns the team around, and it looks as if the Goats might clinch the pennant...their star, Oscar, is horse-napped!

If you love baseball and belly laughs, you'll love
**THE HORSE THAT
PLAYED CENTER FIELD**

SCHOLASTIC INC.

Cover Illustration: Bill Basso

0-590-62011-8